Black Sheep Romeo

(book two of The Royal Romeos series)
by Jenny Gardiner

Copyright © 2016 by Jenny Gardiner

ISBN-13: 978-11944763022

What people are saying about Jenny Gardiner's books:

"A fun, sassy read! A cross between Erma Bombeck and Candace Bushnell, reading Jenny Gardiner is like sinking your teeth into a chocolate cupcake…you just want more."
--Meg Cabot, NY Times bestselling author of Princess Diaries, Queen of Babble and more, on Sleeping with Ward Cleaver

"With a strong yet delightfully vulnerable voice, food critic Abbie Jennings embarks on a soulful journey where her love for banana cream pie and disdain for ill-fitting Spanx clash in hilarious and heartbreaking ways. As her body balloons and her personal life crumbles, Abbie must face the pain and secret fears she's held inside for far too long. I cheered for her the entire way."
--Beth Hoffman, NY Times bestselling author of *Saving CeeCee Honeycutt* on *Slim to None*

"Jenny Gardiner has done it again--this fun, fast-paced book is a great summer read."
--Sarah Pekkanen, NY Times bestselling author of *The Opposite of Me,* on *Slim to None*

"As Sweet as a song and sharp as a beak, *Bite Me* really soars as a memoir about family--children and husbands, feathers and fur--and our capacity to keep loving though life may occasionally bite."
--Wade Rouse, bestselling author of At Least in the City Someone Would Hear Me Scream

Chapter One

FREE-SPIRITED wanderer Lizzie Moretti liked nothing better than to up and move on, which was ironic, considering all her efforts for the past couple of years had gone toward putting down roots. Only those were of the plant variety. By the time they germinated and took hold in the rich soil, she was usually long gone and on to the next farm, where she'd do it all again. Lizzie never stayed in one place for very long and that was fine by her. She loved to see the world and had traveled extensively, typically working on farms in exchange for room and board.

In recent years, she'd planted rice in Indonesia, coffee beans in central Africa, hops in Germany, and was now working with grapes in Italy—although she'd not plant here but instead would help the intensive effort to pick grapes at their peak of ripeness during the impending harvest. She loved the idea of learning how to make wine and had hoped while there to spend a little time looking into her own Italian heritage. Her father's grandparents had emigrated from Italy to America at the turn of the last century. Maybe that's where her wandering came from. No doubt about it, she lived a nomad's life, but it suited her. This time, though, perhaps a lengthy stay in Italy would be a nice way to spend the autumn.

Growing up in a military family, she'd learned the hard way not to get too comfortable in a place and never to establish her own roots because inevitably, her family was displaced each time her father was assigned to yet another military base. They'd had virtually no time to pack and go, leaving little chance even for farewells. Not that she was one for long good-byes anyhow. It was too painful to make good friends only to watch them in the rearview mirror as her mom drove them down the street yet again en route to a new destination—her father having already moved to his newest post.

So she'd learned to appreciate each new place, to live with wings on her feet, always at the ready to take off on a moment's notice. As a young adult, she grew to love this transient existence, with little more than a pack on her back and a pair of Teva sandals or hiking boots on her feet. It made it hard to collect mementos of her travels—after all, there was no place to store them in a forty-pound backpack. Besides, where on earth would she ever put them? Her father had died at the hands of a suicide bomber in Kunduz Province five years ago, and her mother had quickly remarried and moved on with yet another military man—his best friend, to add insult to injury—leaving no true home for Lizzie to return to.

Besides, her lifestyle kept things light and carefree and gave her the chance to follow her impulses and—more importantly—trust her instincts. So far, they hadn't steered her wrong. She'd arrived at a small farm in the Chianti region of Tuscany only a few days ago, hoping to work the grape harvest, then stick around to harvest the olives several weeks later. She'd heard it was a lot of fun, despite being hard work, and she was excited to experience the lush, green countryside of central Italy, the land of fabulous food and wine.

She'd organized the job online, and the host farmer was responsible for ensuring she was legal to participate in the harvest, a coveted job often left only to experts and family members at the large vineyards. But this place was supposedly small, so the opportunity presented itself to her. Her plan was to stick around for maybe six weeks and perhaps work her way toward Australia or New Zealand just in time for the antipodean summertime. Maybe she'd find a coastal area, some sun, sand, and a new land and people to discover.

She was a bit disappointed that this vineyard had no other fellow travelers like her to work the harvest, though. She'd arrived two days ago to learn that the sleeping accommodations were primitive at best: a stone shed with no heat, and judging from the scratching and squeaking sounds around three in the morning, plenty of mice as unwanted roommates. The bathroom was in another shed she had to walk to in the middle of the night and featured a stinky, rudimentary composting toilet.

Alas, it seemed this wasn't going to be a holiday in Tuscany that would involve long, filling, wine-soaked lunches followed by afternoons spent exploring the countryside. Not that she'd expected as much, but a girl could dream, right? She had, however, hoped to be able to wander the region a bit. Her host, an older, grizzled, surly Italian man named Luigi Scalfone, had stated in their e-mail exchange that there would be transportation, but that turned out to be a rusty, decrepit bike with two flat tires.

So far the meals promised her hadn't met basic standards either: they were mostly composed of half-ripened season-end tomatoes that he himself rejected, along with the rotting unsellable vegetables left over from the fields, paired with tins of tuna fish. Even for breakfast. It would be a test of Lizzie's stamina—and stubborn streak— toughing it out for six weeks at this rate. Clearly this agreement wasn't to be a cultural exchange as she'd hoped, but rather a one-sided labor exploitation on Luigi's part.

Over the past few years she'd had mixed experiences wherever she settled in temporarily, but most often things worked out well. Occasionally another farm hand was disagreeable. Sometimes the job description didn't live up to expectations. But for the first time since she'd started as an itinerant helper, she had a bad feeling. First off, Luigi was visibly drunk when she arrived just before dusk on that first evening. She'd hopped off a bus about three miles away and walked the rest of the distance, her heavy pack weighing her down yet the walk doing her good.

She'd passed a gorgeous, very large vineyard anchored by a massive manor home on her way to her destination, and half wondered what it would be like to work there instead. It was so beautiful—and sprawling—from what she could see from a distance. Maybe if she volunteered there as a guest worker she could sleep like a princess on six-hundred-thread-count sheets and after a few hours toiling in the fields, take some time to lounge poolside, or better yet float the afternoon away on a raft, admiring the rolling hillside, peppered with olive groves and vineyards as far as the eye could see. As if. Lizzie could hardly fathom that lifestyle, but she enjoyed the fantasy while her feet hit the pavement, en route to Fattoria Luigi. The word *fattoria* was often the designation in Italy for small working farms and wineries.

When she arrived at the vineyard, she was met by the namesake himself, slurring his words and occupying her personal space, his alcohol-laced breath hot and strong beneath her nose in a manner that made her feel most uncomfortable. He spoke few words, ushered her to the less-than-plush accommodations, and left her to figure out dinner on her own when he passed out in front of the house.

"Welcome to beautiful, hospitable Tuscany," Lizzie muttered as she scrounged in the tiny kitchen for some pasta. She opened the tin of tuna and ate from the can with her fingers before retiring to the privacy of the small hovel she would call home for the next several weeks.

For the first couple of days, she was assigned particularly menial work: sweeping the house, washing dishes, moving wheelbarrows full of rocks, and mucking donkey stalls. Though she was supposed to be working the grape harvest, she was perfectly happy to help out where needed. But she felt terribly unwelcome around her host, who mostly grunted and snapped out short commands to her while he drank until he ended up snoring loudly in unusual locations—slumped over a hay bale in the barn or facedown at the kitchen table.

The way things were shaping up so far, this evidently wasn't going to be one of her favorite destinations. She held out hope that other workers would soon show up to lighten the mood of the place, but not a one had materialized. On the fourth evening, Lizzie took a look at herself in the muted reflection of one of the stainless steel wine tanks in the fermentation room. She had looked better.

Understatement of the year, she thought.

Her large, damp brown eyes poked out from a dirt-encrusted face. Her hair looked like it was going in the direction of Bob Marley. If she didn't pay it some serious attention with soap and water, she'd be sporting dreadlocks by the end of the week. Using what little warm water was afforded her in the outhouse, Lizzie washed her face, scrubbed her long, dark brown hair, plaited it into two pigtail braids, and tucked herself in for bed, ready for a good night's sleep. She hadn't been feeling terrific lately; with a bit of a sore throat and a cough starting to emerge, she felt as if her body was definitely fighting something—maybe just this place—so sleep sounded desperately good.

Soon after she'd lapsed, exhausted, into a deep slumber, she felt the press of a large body against her back. She turned her head and in the darkness made out the grizzled face of her drunken host, whose obvious arousal was insinuating itself into the cushion of her backside. Terrified, she knew she couldn't even scream for help. There was no one here but the two of them, save a host of mice that would be of no help. Where was a fairy godmother when you needed one?

Fortunately, Lizzie had learned long ago to be prepared, so she never went to bed without her minimal belongings together in one place. Thinking quickly, she thrust her elbow hard into Luigi's solar plexus, rolled immediately off the other side of the bed, grabbed her pack and her boots, and took off before Luigi had a chance to regain his breath, writhing as he was in a drunken stupor. She felt no pity for the man as she rushed out the rickety shed door, slamming it tightly behind her. She'd had some squeamish experiences occasionally while traveling as what was essentially a migrant worker, but never had she felt personally violated, and this left her shaken to the core.

As soon as Lizzie was past the sight line of the house, she stopped to put on her hiking boots. She secured her pack onto her back and quickened her pace to get well beyond the fattoria before her disgusting, drunken host could ever catch up with her. Sure she liked to move on at will, but usually it was when she was good and ready, not because she was nearly assaulted.

Once she reached the road, she decided to turn right and follow her tracks the way she'd arrived here days earlier, knowing there would at least be other farms and vineyards along the way. Perhaps a car would pass and she could hitch a ride somewhere—anywhere—just to put some distance between the creepy farmer and herself. Before she could even think about being comfortable, she needed to keep herself safe—the last thing she'd expected to worry about in the welcoming hills of Tuscany.

Chapter Two

MATTEO Romeo arrived back at his family's vineyard just in time for the grape harvest. After a year away from his mother and siblings and the burdensome familial obligations he wasn't sure he wanted to accept as his own, he knew at the very least he had to return for the *vendemmia*, the annual grape harvest that all of Italy anticipates as much as a child would the arrival of Santa on Christmas morning.

And even though Matteo had felt a downright dire need to get away from the disapproving eyes his older brother Sandro—who made him feel like a failure for not wanting to carry on with the family name as expected—Chianti's inexplicable magnetic pull this time of year made it difficult for him to stay away. He was conflicted about returning, though. When it came right down to it, Sandro was the oldest of the five Romeo siblings, and Cantine dei Marchesi Romeo was ultimately going to land in his hands, so why should Matteo put too much of his own blood, sweat, and tears into it?

He asked himself that, but in fact he knew the real reason he'd flown the nest was because of his propensity to scandalize. Be it his mother, his brother, or even the residents of the nearby small, ancestral town of Santa Romeo, they expected Matteo to carry on responsibly and uphold the family name at all times. When he supposedly got a local girl pregnant, everyone was outraged even though ultimately, it was he who was indignant because the baby turned out not to be his. As he'd suspected, his one-off fling with the young woman wasn't what "took," but rather the many nights she'd slept with the married husband of a local schoolteacher had.

Matteo didn't really think he deserved to be lumped into the scandal between the lot of them; he'd just had sex with her after the town festa celebrating last year's grape harvest. One time. And sure, once was all it took; he knew that. Eventually he realized she was much further along than would be humanly possible had he been the baby daddy, and he coerced a confession from her. That's when he decided it was time to put some distance between him and this suffocating one-horse town that had owned him his entire life.

He wasn't sure when he'd return to the ancestral fold and surprised even himself when the yearning for that sense of belonging that only came from family and *terroir* began to stir deep within him. He'd spent the past year of his life wandering. He was lucky he had the unlimited funds to do so. And he did it with a vengeance, traveling first class to the far reaches of the world, first China, then Thailand, next to Africa, and eventually to Central and South America. He'd enjoyed himself immensely, staying at top-tier hotels and occasionally even bedding down beautiful women in a few of those choice destinations along the way. But with the vendemmia looming, his heart was calling him back home, despite himself.

He arrived days before the harvest was to begin, just in time for a huge family Sunday lunch.

"The prodigal son!" his sister Valentina squealed, running to embrace him when she saw him drop his bags on the terrace where a long table was set for the meal. "I knew you'd come home for the harvest. I just knew you couldn't stay away from your favorite sister."

Matteo stood back to take a good, long look at his younger sister. "Don't you mean my only sister?" he said with a grin. "Ahhh, Valentina. It's hard to imagine how it's possible, but you've become even more beautiful in my absence. I've come back to keep the men away from you." He kissed her cheeks.

She waved him away. "Don't you dare keep them away from me. I need all the help I can get to attract them. Mamma," she called to her mother, who was inside putting the finishing touches on the meal, "you'll never guess what the cat dragged in."

"I hope it's not another snake," his mother Fabiana said, looking up as she walked onto the terrace. As soon as she saw her son, she gasped, wiped her hands on her dress, and ran to him. "Matteo! *Finalemente, mio figlio.* Finally, my son, you have returned home." She kissed his cheeks and hugged him fiercely.

"Mamma," he said, inhaling the aroma from platters of food being placed on the table by staff. "I couldn't stay away from your cooking." He rubbed his belly.

"I knew I could lure you home, my sweet boy." She kissed him again. "Sit, eat."

"Did you just call for your sweet boy?" Matteo's brother Sandro laughed as he came out to the terrace, only to see Matteo being smothered with hugs from their mother.

"Look who's come home!" Fabiana said.

Sandro stared at his brother, eventually giving a short nod. "Matteo."

The two of them could almost be twins, both in age and appearance. They shared the same wavy dark hair, though Matteo's was a little shorter, and their mother's warm, brown eyes. Sandro had a moustache and goatee, providing the distinguishing factor between the two.

Matteo nodded back. "Sandro."

The last thing Matteo had wanted was an immediate standoff with his brother. They'd long been good friends, though they parted ways when it came to family expectations, which was why Matteo left in the first place. When his brother expressed such outrage at him for supposedly getting the local girl pregnant, that was it for Matteo.

The two men looked at each other for a brief moment until the standoff was broken by a gorgeous, tall, blond woman with an unmistakable American accent.

"It's about time," said his brother's girlfriend, Taylor McFarland. "I was beginning to think it was something I'd said!" She enveloped him in a hug, then seemed to remember the obligatory cheek kisses so threw them in for good measure. It wasn't long after Taylor took up with Sandro that Matteo and his brother had their falling-out and Matteo fled Italy.

"Taylor, you look as magnificent as ever," Matteo said. "I don't know why you put up with my brother when you could have me instead."

She laughed. "Thanks, but I like the hardship cases. More of a challenge."

"Well, you've got a challenge with Sandro, no doubt," he said, shaking his head. "He's lucky you took pity on him."

"Everyone, sit," Fabiana said as they found their seats

and settled in for their feast. "Sandro, pour the wine. Lorenzo, Francesco, Tomasso, and Giorgio are coming late for lunch today. It will be perfect to have all of my children together at last. What a way to start the vendemmia."

Matteo looked at his family members, who were already gathered around the table, happy to see them yet apprehensive after being away for so long. He wondered where exactly he would fit in now that he'd stepped even further away from the fold.

What a way to start the vendemmia, indeed.

Chapter Three

SOMEHOW walking along the beautiful Tuscan roads by day held a more appealing charm than they did on a dark, moonless night. The one good thing was that Lizzie would know of a car's approach in advance: between the focused beams of headlights and the sound of an engine on an otherwise silent night, at least she knew she'd not end up run over by a passing vehicle. Of course, the chances of this dwindled significantly because not one approached in the hour or so she'd been walking.

And while the heft of the pack on her back seemed less significant during that late-day meander to the fattoria, now it felt burdensome. It didn't help matters that she hadn't taken the time to get properly dressed and was still in her pajamas—if you could even call them that. More like skimpy shorts and a sleeveless T-shirt, sans bra. But at this hour, it obviously didn't matter. Clearly no one was going to see her because no one, but no one seemed to be out on this very lonely stretch of two-way road.

She tried to mentally backtrack to recall what she'd seen as she walked this way days earlier. She remembered walking past that very large vineyard, but aside from that, not a whole lot, maybe another fattoria, perhaps an *agriturismo* (a farmhouse) or two set far back from the road. But she'd not find anyone at home or at least awake and willing to help out at one of those bed and breakfast types of farms. And in the dark, nothing looked the same.

Worse still, she'd initially arrived at a bus stop, so retracing her steps to where she began wouldn't help her right now. There wouldn't be a bus for many hours. She was tired, her back had started to ache, and she was nursing a sore throat and a simmering rage at the man whose predatory actions led her to be stranded in the middle of nowhere.

Moments like this almost made her want to return home. Almost. But then she remembered there really wasn't a home to which she could return. She and her mother hadn't spoken much in years. They both dealt with their grief in entirely different ways after her father's death, and it seemed her mother's was to find a new man far too quickly. Lizzie resented it. Her only other immediate relative was an older brother who had decided to enlist in the military in his father's memory, to honor him, he claimed. Lizzie was so upset at that she could barely speak to him. It was bad enough she'd lost her father; now her brother had put himself in harm's way as well. It was too much for her to deal with, so she walked away from family, from that which caused her the most hurt. It was easier that way.

And now she found herself walking again—this time, briskly—away from yet another unpleasant episode in her world. Normally she wasn't one to dwell on the past, but here, in the middle of the night, with no place to rest her head, she felt the weight of life's insults bearing down on her, until all she wanted to do was sit down and cry. But the side of a winding country road was not the place to do that, where she risked not only chance encounters with cars but also wild boars and even venomous snakes.

She felt a drop of moisture on her arm, then another

and another, and within minutes a soaking rain descended upon her. She fumbled behind her for her rain poncho, which had been secured to the outside of her pack, but it wasn't there. Somehow in her haste to escape, it must have unsnapped and fallen off. Damn that Luigi. The chill autumn air had been tolerable until accompanied by a drenching rain, and soon her teeth began to chatter and her body shivered beneath the assault.

She'd once been stuck in a typhoon on a cargo ship after hitching a ride to cross the Indian Ocean—a pretty miserable experience. At least she'd found shelter from the powerful storm, even if she was violently ill from the churning waves. She'd been trapped in Burundi during a coup attempt when all routes out of the country were shut down. But she was under cover, warm and dry, albeit a bit frightened.

Right now, though, vulnerable and violated from what she'd barely escaped, alone in the cold rain on a dark, lonely stretch of mountainous road with no place to go, well, she felt weak. Which she hated more than anything, because the one thing Lizzie Moretti wasn't was weak. When the going got rough, she figured out how to smooth out the path forward.

She realized she'd been looking down while walking, making sure she didn't step on something that would cause her to roll an ankle or fall into the ditch just off the edge of the pavement. And so when she looked up, she was surprised to see some lights in the distance, high up on a hill.

She crossed the road and walked another quarter mile till she saw a sign for the sprawling property to which the lights belonged: the large vineyard she'd seen on her way to the fattoria, days earlier. Cantine dei Marchesi Romeo, the illuminated sign said. She wasn't up on her wines, so she had no idea about this vineyard, but it looked like the kind of place a girl could wander around and find a bit of shelter without being detected: precisely what she needed right about now.

She turned into the driveway, only to find a gate tightly shut. But a little security gate was hardly enough to keep a determined Lizzie from finding a way around it.

She pulled out her phone and turned on the flashlight, focusing it on the far side of the strong iron fencing that buffered the entrance, and noticed that it barely extended past the two tall stone pillars that secured the wrought iron fencing in place on either side of the gate. Beyond each pillar was a low stone wall, which posed little challenge for Lizzie to breach.

She removed her pack and hoisted it over the edge of the wall, where it fell with a soft thud. Next she shimmied her way down the side of the wall, some five feet below the level of the roadway, and landed on her feet. Dusting off her hands, she grabbed her pack and threw it back on, snapping the waistband and chest strap in place.

The easiest route to the property would be straight up the grand Italian cypress-lined driveway. It likely wound along the hillside a good three-quarters of a mile, but she'd be easily detected if there were people tasked with guarding the property at night. Instead she chose to navigate her way up the terraced hillside, through occasional stands of trees, hoping for no encounters with any Italian wild things. As she fought to secure her footing in the slick mud while scaling the hill, she couldn't help but think she'd had enough of wild things in Italy for one night.

By the time she'd clambered up the steep, uneven slopes, she had slipped so many times she wasn't sure if any of her flesh remained unmarred by a coating of mud. She'd gone without a shower plenty of times in her nomadic life and was accustomed to bouts with no water to bathe at the ready. But she was hard-pressed to think of a time in which she craved a shower—followed by a long, hot soak in a bathtub—more than now. And it was hard to imagine which was worse: the slick of mud on just about every exposed part of her skin or the cold rain that caused her teeth to chatter almost uncontrollably.

She kept an eye on the enormous manor home, tracking far enough away from it to remain undetected in case someone looked out a window. Though Lord knows what they'd see as fog had enshrouded the hills enough to obscure her movements by now. Eventually she stumbled upon an old stone toolshed, mercifully larger than the tiny stone shack in which she'd been relegated at Fattoria Luigi. She opened the creaky door, peering into the darkness. She reached into a side pocket where she'd secured her phone from the rain, pulled it out, and turned on the flashlight.

It was an amazingly clean and organized space, the concrete floors free of dirt and debris, and tools and supplies neatly stored on shelves or hung on hooks on the walls. The shed was about the size of one of those super-huge four-car garages she'd seen back in the States. It was downright spacious, and against the far wall was a somewhat tattered sofa that looked to be impossibly comfortable at this point. If only there was a little bit of heat, she'd be perfectly content. Well, make that content enough to get by. Her own sleeping bag was soaked through by now, so she was going to have to curl up and hope her body heat would do the trick.

Lizzie pushed the door shut, leaving her phone light on to illuminate the space so she could unpack the contents of her backpack. Most of her belongings were sopping wet, and she draped them across any surface she could find in the hope they might dry out a bit by morning. To the hooks on the wall, she suspended the two bras and the four pairs of panties she traveled with. She spread out her sleeping bag on a large worktable next to her two pairs of hiking socks, then stripped off her soaking pajamas, which she hung on the inside doorknob.

Her eyes scanned the shelves of supplies that ran along one wall until they fell on what looked like a large canvas drop cloth on a high shelf. She reached for a pole with a hook attached that hung on the wall and used it to pull down the cloth. She opened it up, gave it a quick once-over to be sure it wasn't disgustingly filthy, and decided it would simply have to do as she folded it in half for extra warmth. At this point, dry was going to have to be good enough and clean a concept for another day.

She grabbed her phone and the tarp, curled her naked self on the dingy sofa, and pulled the cloth over her shivering body. She'd catch a few hours of sleep and be up and out of there long before anyone discerned she was usurping their shed. As she nodded off to sleep, she realized that sometimes it took life being boiled to its very essence to feel truly grateful for what little you have: a roof over her head, protection from the elements, and something soft to finally put your head on. Things had gotten as bad as they could and now they could only get better.

Chapter Four

MATTEO'S body clock was out of whack. Try as he might, he couldn't seem to stay asleep for more than an hour or two without waking. A strong rainstorm rolled in long after the sun had set, which meant the harvest would be postponed for a day or two while the grapes dried and he could sleep in. It rained hard overnight and he thought he'd sleep well with the hypnotizing drumbeat of rainfall on the roof. Instead Matteo tossed and turned until at last, around dawn, he decided to get up and wander the property to refamiliarize himself with his old life. Maybe it could help him discern whether or not he wanted this to be part of his reinvented life.

He didn't even bother to grab a quick espresso from the kitchen. Instead he threw on his Barbour jacket to fend off the morning chill—a favorite purchase before leaving London, the last stop on his world tour—and slipped quietly out the back door and across the terrace, where he took in the view of the Romeo family property that stretched for miles. Fog from the night's rain had settled into the valleys, covering those low-lying areas like nature's undergarments, obscuring bits and pieces he might like to see more of. Mother Nature was a bit of a tease.

Yet as he took in the entire panorama, he was pleased to see that the season's earthen hues of ochre, sienna, and russet had begun to eclipse summertime's palette of greens. The grape leaves in a few parts of the vineyard were giving way to a more seductive Titian red, their blushing vines lined up in orderly rows. Far in the distance, the old-growth olive trees sparkled a silvery green as the sun crested the horizon. The patchwork of color from all that sprang from the earth here made the countryside appear as if it were a comfortable quilt he longed to curl up beneath.

Despite himself, he felt a tug of belonging to this place that absence somehow hadn't erased. He closed his eyes and just breathed, relaxing into the moment, reveling in that sense of being one with this plot of earth his family had claimed for so many centuries. And no matter how much he satisfied his wanderlust, he'd be lying if he didn't admit that something about home called to him and drew him back here.

The big question was this: sure the vineyard itself might appeal, but what about those in charge of the place? Could he deal with Sandro's alpha doggedness? Was the perfection of this place enough to enable him to put up with his pain-in-the-ass brother? He shook his head to clear the thoughts away and decided to meander around the property. He didn't want to think about any of that right now. After all, no reason to spoil a near-perfect start to the day.

Matteo descended the marble staircase that led to gardens. He strolled past fountains where mythological creatures made of travertine stone spouted water that fed a small pond from which a small green frog emerged.

He loved the many surprises nature gifted him when he explored the estate. He let his feet lead him toward one of his favorite spots on the property: a field of *girasoli*, the tall, beautiful sunflowers that thrive throughout Tuscany.

It was because of him this field even existed. As a

child, he would beg his mother to take him to see the massive fields of sunflowers that peppered the Tuscan countryside, where tens of thousands of cheery, golden, floral faces reached toward the sun for sustenance during the sweltering summer months. Finally his mother persuaded his father to plant a field of sunflowers so Matteo could enjoy them all day long without their having to drive elsewhere. Which he did, often traipsing amidst the tall stalks, playing hide-and-seek with his siblings, or sometimes even taking a book into the field to nestle beneath the shade of the tall flowers.

This field would lie fallow until next June or July when the sunflowers returned for their joyful visit. Now only a few remaining holdouts—the late bloomers—stood somewhat erect. Their undying optimism that the sun would care for them even as colder weather crept in like a thief stealing away the summer warmth was reassuring to him. Matteo could relate to those flowers that came into their own so much later; he felt a bit like a latecomer to the Romeo wine world himself, having tolerated his brother's insistence that only he could run things all this time.

Gah! He'd promised himself he'd stop ruminating on Sandro, but it wasn't till he heard a familiar grunt and spied the scrawny tail of a wild boar scurrying away from a section of the vineyard that his mind made the leap to a more interesting subject matter. He shouted to shoo the large, bristly creature away. Wild boar loved to eat grapes, and anyone working in the wine business was happy for hunting season to begin to thin out the herd and protect the crop.

"*Va'via!*" he said with a dramatic sweep of his arms and stomp of his feet. "Get lost, or I'll turn you into a piping-hot plate of *cinghiale*." He was referring to Tuscany's most famous dish: a delicious, comforting meat stew made with boar meat.

Cinghiale, he thought, his stomach giving off a loud rumble and reminding him he'd not yet eaten. Yet another thing he longed for during his travels. As much as he loved to indulge in street foods unique to each culture he'd spent time in, he couldn't help but yearn for the familiarity of his mamma's home cooking, pappardelle al cinghiale in particular. Served with a glass of Romeo wines' prized Chianti Classico Riserva, of course.

He walked on as a hare leapt away upon hearing the rustle of leaves underfoot. As he navigated his way through a section of vineyard he noticed a grape rake haphazardly left on the ground.

"Huh. My responsible brother is not overseeing his farmhands," he said with a grimace. "Or maybe he's just lowered his impossibly high standards."

He grabbed the tool and headed toward the toolshed to return the item to its proper place. As he approached, he heard a strange sound coming from inside, almost a kinder, gentler version of the squealing grunts of a wild boar. The door appeared to be shut tightly, so it was unlikely that an animal had slipped in overnight. Though perhaps something had gotten into the shed during the day and remained inside, undetected.

Just to be safe, he raised the rake over his head as he carefully opened the door and tiptoed in. The last thing he'd want to do was scare some wild creature that would charge him. The problem was it was pretty dark inside the shed, with only two one-foot-square window openings to allow light in, and it was still just dawn.

The noise grew louder as he crossed the threshold, and he crept with the stealth of a cat burglar into the building, which naturally, was pristine because, well, his brother was in charge. He suddenly heard a snort, which frightened him.

"Ahh!" he shouted.

"Ahhhhhh!" a high-pitched voice screamed back.

"Omigod, don't move," he said, his pitchfork at the ready.

"You touch me and I swear to God I will kick you in the nuts so hard your teeth will rattle."

Well, crap. Those were words that would put the fear of God into any self-respecting man.

Chapter Five

WHOEVER it was who owned that scream and the even more shocking words stood up. Matteo's eyes had adjusted to the dim room, and he could easily make out a young woman, her apparently naked body draped with what looked like a canvas farm tarp.

"Who are you and what are you doing here?" he said.

"Who are you and what are you going to do with me?" she said, as she stood slightly squatting like a sumo wrestler while assessing his next move.

"I asked you first!"

"I asked you second!"

"Look, sweetheart," he said. "You've got about three seconds to sit down before I call the police on you." He knew his phone didn't work in this part of the estate, but she didn't know that.

"Sweetheart?" she said. "Cute. Who are you, Frank Sinatra or something? Where's your Rat Pack?"

He glared at her and gave her a good, solid once-over: from the top of her bedraggled head of hair to the tips of what looked like a pair of very muddy feet. She still stood, defying his orders, her arms quasi-outstretched (with elbows holding up the tarp) as if ready to karate chop him.

"What are you doing in my shed?"

"Your shed?" she said, her face growing red. Or perhaps it was the early morning sun illuminating what looked like dry red clay on her countenance.

"You're like a parrot, repeating my words back to me. Enough with the imitation," he said. "I want to know why you're trespassing on my property."

One thing Sandro had achieved with a great degree of success was to instill in his younger brother a level of paranoia about spies and intruders wanting to learn the secrets to his family's award-winning wines. During harvest time, aside from family, the estate was staffed only with workers who returned year after year, people the Romeos could count on to be honest and trustworthy. Strangers showing up in the middle of the night just as the harvest was about to get underway? No can do. Something was up with this mystery woman, and he was going to get to the bottom of it.

He glanced at the wall and saw a string of undergarments dangling from hooks and tools mounted there for storage. As his eyes adjusted to the dimness, he noticed a pair of bright purple panties and couldn't help but think how much he'd like to pluck that grape that fit into those things. Which was so not the proper thought to have pop into his head while encountering a rogue, well, whatever she was camping out in their toolshed.

The young woman tugged the tarp up higher against her chest as if she were wearing a ball gown rather than a dirty stretch of canvas. Her bare shoulders were exposed, revealing tan lines that betrayed the body of a laborer: clearly she'd not been lounging in a bikini any time recently, what with the farmer's tan and lithe, sculpted biceps she sported. Matteo struggled to tamp down thoughts of running his hands across the soft white skin of her upper back, her strong back that looked as if it had been working intensely for a long time.

"I'm not bothering anyone," she said, which was just about the last thing he expected from her. Surely someone caught out hiding on another person's property would fall on her sword in apology instead of digging in defensively. He recognized her accent as American and wondered if she knew she risked having her visa rescinded for trespassing on Romeo property.

"From where I stand it seems that you're an intruder," he said. "One who I suspect is here to spy on our harvest."

She glared at him. "Paranoid, much?" One side of her upper lip lifted in a sneer. "Or is it that you're an elitist pig who can't just let a girl seek shelter from the rain on a cold night?"

What a contemptuous little thing!

"Frankly, your needs are not my concern. But I do want to know what you're doing here before I call the police and have you thrown in jail."

"Jail?" she said, her face falling. "Why would you do that? You'll get me kicked out of the country, and then I'll have no place to go."

"Perhaps you should have thought about that before you helped yourself to our hospitality, unbidden."

He wanted nothing more than to turn her out, or over to the local *polizia*, though he figured the police couldn't really be bothered with a dirty, wet vagrant. They'd probably give her an espresso and drop her at the nearest train station after fining her handsomely. And judging by her appearance, the money to pay notoriously steep Italian fines wasn't something she had at the ready, if at all. Nor was the money for a train anywhere. But he knew he was going to deal with a load of shit from Sandro—who tended to border on paranoid when it came to his grapes and his harvest and the notion of spies amongst them—if he didn't get rid of her pronto.

The woman slowly shuffled her feet sideways toward her dangling panties, evidently concerned about his next move.

"Would you at least put down the weaponry?" she said, pointing to the rake he continued to hold aloft as if ready to strike.

Matteo winced. He didn't want to come across as *that* type of man. Someone who would hurt a woman, ever. He quickly put down the tool, then noticed her teeth were chattering.

"Look, um, whoever you are," he said, taking a step toward her. "You look like you need to warm up a bit."

She flinched, taking a step back. "I'm fine," she said a little too forcefully. "If I can just get my clothes on, I'll be out of here and leave you alone to possessively guard your spider-filled toolshed against marauding invaders."

He frowned at her ungrateful remarks. "Listen, lady," he said. "I don't know who you are, and for all I know you're a plant from the competition here to spy on Romeo wines. So, yeah, I do want you out of here."

She rolled her eyes. "Do I look like a spy?" she said. "I mean, really, take a look at me." She reached out and plucked her purple panties from the closest hook.

Matteo glanced to see her bra was just out of reach, and that didn't disappoint him terribly because yeah, he wouldn't mind taking a good look at her.

"Spies come in all shapes and sizes," he said. "And colors, judging by those things." He nodded at her panties and grinned.

"Oh, gee, thanks. So you've got a thing for wet

panties?" She blanched as soon as she said it.

He smiled for the first time, a broad smile revealing straight white teeth. "As a matter of fact, they're my favorite kind."

"Ha, ha. Very funny. Perv."

Matteo's eyes grew wide. "Sorry, honey. Whoever you are, whatever reason you're here, you've disrupted the perfectly lovely walk I was taking on the estate. And now I'm stuck trying to figure out what to do with the likes of you. Obviously you don't belong here but you seem to think it's your birthright to be here nonetheless. So I would suggest you collect your things—"

"Crazy request but do you suppose I *could put some clothes on*?" she said, shouting the last bit for emphasis. "Or would you prefer I just leave here stark naked?"

He lowered his head toward her and raised his eyebrows. "Do you really want an answer to that question?"

She sniffed. "Like I said: perv. Do you mind?"

She held the edge of the tarp between her teeth to secure it in place while she used one hand to try to pull on her underwear, not particularly gracefully, shifting her feet like a bad dancer.

Matteo was anxious to see how she'd get that bra on. *This ought to be good.* Shy of lending a hand, he thought perhaps he should just pull up a chair and sit back and enjoy the show.

"Is this how they do it here in your country?" she asked, scowling at him. "Just gawk at the woman in distress?"

He shrugged. "Huh. Based on your reaction to being caught red-handed, I wasn't under the impression you were in distress. You came across more like indignant, maybe even rude, so I didn't realize you needed help."

"Look," she said, reaching out a trembling hand to grab a lime-green bra suspended from a spade. "I'm sorry if I took up your precious, unoccupied toolshed last night. Now, if you'll let me dress with a modicum of privacy—"

"Absolutely," he said, crossing his arms across his chest and staring at her. He wanted so badly to watch her put that bra on. He just knew at some point something would slip, and it had been awhile since he'd glimpsed anything as tantalizing as this grungy-looking woman—half-covered in dirt, her hair clumped this way and that. He couldn't for the life of him figure out what it was that intrigued him about her, but it did.

"Well, then turn around already." She glared at him and motioned with her hand to spin around and face the door. Clearly she wasn't as impressed with him as he was curious about her. He slowly shifted his body till his back was turned toward her. He could only hear the rustling of the drop cloth, then the sound of fabric against skin. Damn, she must have been putting everything on. There went his entertainment for the morning. He was kind of hoping for a seductive, slow dressing, sort of like a reverse striptease.

"Is the coast clear yet?" he said after it sounded like she had plenty of time to do what she needed to do. She just grunted.

He turned around to see her quickly stuffing the rest of her dangling belongings into a backpack that had been stuck in a corner.

"Hope none of those spiders you mentioned decided to hitchhike their way into your pack," he said. She jumped back for a second, only to then cast a glare his way.

"Of course you're trying to freak me out," she said, continuing to pack as fast as possible.

"Hey. You're lucky it was I who surprised you and not a frightened porcupine," he said. "The *istrici* sometimes find their way into this shed at night. Would have been perfectly fitting, one prickly creature to another. Only with them, one false move and you'd have been begging me to pluck spines from your backside."

He had to admit the idea of servicing her bottom, which looked pretty close to perfect now that he could see it outlined in the form-fitting yoga pants she'd slipped on, wasn't at all off-putting, and he smiled despite himself. He'd been having such a peaceful morning before he stumbled upon this intruder. This filthy, surly, bedraggled, and surprisingly easy-on-the-eyes interloper. And somehow he wasn't the least bit upset about the disruption. He let out a short laugh.

"What's so funny?" she said with a snarl.

"I was just thinking how much fun that could have been."

"By all means, enjoy a bit of humor at my expense," she said. "Now if you could hand me my boots right by the door, I'll get on my way then."

He turned and saw a pair of soaking-wet hiking boots in a corner and picked them up. "You can't wear these things," he said. "They're saturated."

"I've dealt with worse problems in my life." Their hands touched as she reached out to grab hold of them. She was shaking.

"What's with the tremor?" he asked her.

She held out her hand, which would not stay steady.

"I'm just a little bit cold," she said. "Nothing I can't fix. I'll warm up once I get moving."

"Yeah, especially with a pair of sopping boots." He really shouldn't care about her but it seemed wrong to send someone out on a cold morning chilled to the bone.

"Maybe a sip of water will help me feel better," she said. "You got any?"

He pulled a bottle from his pocket and passed it to her. "You're shaking like you're freezing, but your hand feels like it's on fire." He decided to risk a punch to the face by placing the palm of his hand to her forehead. "You've got a fever. Your skin feels like the pavement on a summer afternoon." He could feel the heat pulsating off of her.

She waved a dismissive hand at him as she sat on the sofa to pull on her boots. They didn't want to go on easily, wet as they were. "Look, I'm fine."

"Why don't I get you inside, let you take a warm shower, and we can scare up some clean clothes for you. My sister Valentina is about your size—I'm sure she has something warm for you to borrow." He couldn't believe he even suggested that, bringing her into the house where Sandro was sure to see her and freak out on him.

"The problem with borrowing is I'll be long gone," she said. "And no place to put it, and no way to return it. I prefer to remain unencumbered, thanks."

She stood up, grabbed her pack, lifted it onto her shoulders, and snapped the front belts into place across her stomach and chest. Matteo felt a tinge of envy toward that chest strap.

"Thanks for the kindest of hospitality," she said. "Here's hoping our paths never cross a—"

Only she never finished her sentence as her body crumpled to the floor, a heap of irritable, self-righteous, annoying, and adorable, looking frighteningly lifeless on the concrete floor.

Chapter Six

HER panties were wet. And not in a good way. She felt like crap. She was so cold she couldn't contain the shivering in her body, and she wanted desperately to unearth her toothbrush to scrub away what felt like an infantry brigade that must have taken up space in her mouth. Not to mention a glass of water—nowhere to be found—would be amazing. What she would give to be cozied up before a warm fireplace sipping hot cocoa; clean and toasty and well-fed would be a nice option. Well-rested as well.

Instead she stood shivering in a crap shack, half-naked with a veritable police interrogation underway conducted by the jerk guy who couldn't just humor her and let her get on her way. Finally—*finally!*—he seemed to warm up to the idea of letting her just get out and go. Wasn't her first choice because, well, she hadn't figured that out yet, the where-to-go-next piece of the puzzle. Plus, she wasn't exactly feeling her best. She chalked that up to the chill she couldn't seem to shake all night long. She was cold, hungry, and thirsty: according to *Maslow's Hierarchy of Needs* she was decidedly not feeling life's abundance.

She figured if she could get herself onto a bus, maybe get to a hostel in Florence for a night, she could at least take a hot shower and find a bed with sheets and even a blanket. And perhaps, if everyone was really quiet—though what were the chances of that in a hostel?—she could sleep the whole night through and not leave until they kicked her out for cleaning time. If, just if.

She threw her pack on, ready to get away from the grumpy guy as soon as her feet could take her. "Here's hoping our paths never cross a—"

But she never got the rest of the word out, because her mouth felt like it was filled with cotton and she was seeing purple and then she wasn't seeing anything at all.

"Hey, lady," she heard a voice say. Then she felt the sharp sting of a hand on her face and she opened her eyes, squinting. Through hazy slits, she could make out the face of that surly guy, right up on hers only inches away. And did he just slap her?

"Lady," he said, muttering out loud. "*Mamma mia*, I don't even know her name. And now I've got this strange woman passed out on the floor. Thank God she got dressed. I'd have really been in trouble if she were totally naked in a heap on the ground. What am I going to do? Am I supposed to do CPR? Oh God. Sandro is going to flip out."

"Lizard," she said in a rasp.

He put his ear to her mouth. "You're alive! *Merda!* What did you say? Lizard? You must be hallucinating."

"Lizzie," she said.

"Mamma mia," he said again. "Could you tell me your name?"

"Lizzie," she said in a raspy voice.

"Your mother called you Lizard? What a strange name. *Mi chiamo* Matteo. I'd shake hands but, well, never mind. Listen, Lizard. You're going to be okay. I'm going to get you to the house and we'll call the doctor for you, all right?"

"Lizzie," she said again.

"I know, I know. Lizard. I got it. Must be some strange sort of American name," he said, once again touching her forehead. "You're on fire. I need to get you to the manor home. We'll deal with your trespassing matter later, but for now, if you can just extend your arm, I'll help you up. First, let me get this thing off of your back."

He unbuckled her waist strap and carefully unsnapped the one that spanned her stretched-tight T-shirt; then he pulled off the backpack. "We'll deal with that thing later. Though I don't know what you'd want in there anyway. The whole thing smells disgusting and it's wet all the way through."

Lizzie lay in a haze of sedation on the floor, alternately shivering and drifting off, hearing the man—Matteo, kind of a hot Italian name—talking like he'd never seen someone pass out before. Well, Lizzie hadn't either, for that matter. But she'd like to think she'd be less frantic than he sounded.

"Crap, if only my phone worked out here, I could call for help. Or at least Google what to do when a stranger passes out in your shed. I'm sure this is not the first time such a thing has happened. Maybe she's on drugs. Maybe she needed to pay for her drug habit so she agreed to spy on Romeo wines. Crap, crap, crap. Sandro is going to go ballistic."

He propped Lizzie up in a seated position and she

slumped forward. She probably looked like those very ancient people in nursing homes whose heads are down near their navels while seated in a wheelchair. He reached out his arms again. "Okay, Lizard. So now we're going to get you the rest of the way up and then I'm going to get you to drape your arm across my shoulder and lean into me, and I'll bear as much of your weight as possible. It's not too far of a walk."

Lizzie felt like she was yelling at him but no words were coming out. Why did he keep calling her Lizard? What was wrong with him?

She was a limp rag doll and was happy to let him lead the way. She was always bad at ballroom dancing because she could never let the man lead. Maybe the key to it was passing out cold—then she could be easily manipulated into any sort of position necessary. In this case, it was wrapped around the man like she was a giant bandage plastered on his body. In and out of conscious thinking, she worried fleetingly that if he caught one whiff of her breath he might go down cold himself.

"You with me, Lizard?" he was saying to her. She didn't know why she never thought to call herself Lizard before. She was sort of getting used to it. Lizard. It had a certain cachet to it. It almost seemed a little badass. Though not as if she could be seen as badass while being dragged around like a cadaver.

"So this is the field of sunflowers my mamma made my papa plant for me. I know it sounds weird but it made me very happy. Girasoli—that's 'sunflowers' in Italian—have always made me feel great joy, and my mamma knew that." He continued on through the fields. "Once I found a mamma cat and her kittens here, just on the edge of these trees. I brought them to my bedroom where they stayed for days until I realized that cats needed litter boxes. Mamma about killed me. But we did keep the kittens. There's always a place for cats on a farm when you have to deal with rodents."

The man all of a sudden wouldn't stop babbling. She was learning his life story but her head ached and her chest did even more so. Every time she tried to breathe her lungs screamed at her.

She could feel heat and sweat generating along the man's neckline. It was chilly outside still, but the poor guy was working up a lather just dragging her wherever he was taking her. She made a mental note to lose a few pounds in case anyone ever had to lug her around again. Embarrassing!

"This fountain," he said, pointing at a large burnished statue rendering of Bacchus surrounded by some sort of mythological party animals. "It was a gift from Sophia Loren to my father back in her heyday. She loved his wines. He loved her curves."

"Water," Lizzie said. But it seemed he couldn't hear whatever she said, which was convenient yet inconvenient. Because in the course of her mental meanderings, she'd thought he was a selfish, mean sourpuss. Yet that changed and she thought him a really lovely, thoughtful man. But she didn't want him to know either of her impressions of him. It didn't matter anyhow—she'd be out of here in a matter of hours and would not cross paths with him ever again.

They stopped at the base of a flight of steps. Lizzie opened her eyes a little against the sunlight that had spread across the horizon by now. She wasn't quite sure where she was being taken but the view was resplendent, with undulating hills in shades of green and splashes of autumnal auburns as well. Matteo sat her down and rested her against the steps and called for help.

"By now staff should be up and working," he said, dusting off his hands as if he'd just finished digging a grave or something equally physically taxing. God, she hoped he wasn't going to dig her a grave.

"*Aiuto!* Help."

Two men came immediately along with a woman who smelled like fresh bread. Lizzie wanted to follow her wherever she was going. Fresh bread sounded divine.

The men talked back and forth in Italian, she presumed, about body-carrying strategies judging by their dramatic hand gestures and a demonstrative wipe of sweat across a brow, and Lizzie again vowed to get rid of that extra weight she must've gained.

The woman clucked and lamented in Italian so Lizzie wasn't quite sure what she was saying. Next thing she knew, the three men were carrying her up the wide flight of steps, a lumpy yet capable ride. The three of them continued into the large house, the smell of bread taunting her, so close but yet so far.

Finally they placed her atop a bed in a darkened room. By now her teeth chattered uncontrollably and she wanted desperately to submerge beneath whatever the soft bedding was beneath her bones. But this Matteo fellow had other plans because moments later he helped her into a bathroom, where the woman had been running a hot bath. And never had Lizzie felt such tears of joy spring from her eyes as now.

"Allegra has been with us since we were children. She

gave me every bath I had until I'd outgrown them. She's going to help clean you up and get you to bed. I'll be back to check on you after I call the doctor."

Lizzie couldn't generate enough concern to even be embarrassed to be a full-grown woman being bathed by what was basically an aged nanny. She lifted her arms as Allegra directed her and, with the help of the strong woman, was helped out of her damp clothes and into the cocoon of warmth the tub offered her. She couldn't believe how filled with joy she was just to feel the sultry water wash over her. Allegra started with a soft washcloth to her face, then her arms, and worked her way down her entire body. She then took the spray nozzle and aimed it at her hair, working it into a lather and massaging her scalp with professional dexterity. If Lizzie didn't feel so horrible she'd feel downright wonderful.

Soon Allegra helped her to stand as she rinsed her thoroughly and helped her step out of the bath. She enveloped her in one of the thickest, warmest towels to ever touch her body. Warm towels—what a novel idea. She made a mental note to one day aspire to own a towel warmer.

The steam and the aroma of citrus from the shampoo filled the room with warmth and caring and she felt so very loved. Which was weird, because she'd just had a complete stranger scrubbing dirt off her body. And now she was toweling her off and slipping a soft pink silk satin camisole over her head and helping her step into matching sleep shorts. If she didn't feel so awful, she'd feel wonderful in such indulgent sleepwear, not something that existed in her world.

Allegra helped seat Lizzie before a large mirror and

proceeded to dry her hair before escorting her back to the plush bed she'd sat atop ever-so-fleetingly half an hour ago. The woman tucked her beneath layers of down and soft sheets, then even scratched her fingers along her scalp, a sweet sign of affection that left Lizzie feeling even more grateful for the kindness of strangers. Even the grumpy one showed he could be a nice person. It helped to make up for the trauma that led her here in the first place. Barely.

But how was she going to sneak out of here now that she was happily ensconced in the most sublimely snug bed she'd ever had the good fortune to burrow into? Couldn't she just hibernate here for the winter?

Chapter Seven

PNEUMONIA. Lizard—he still couldn't get over what a ridiculous name she had—had a bad case of bacterial pneumonia, according to Dr. Sarducci, who seemed most certain of this fact. And a large goose egg on the side of her head where she went down, but he wasn't concerned about that. He'd left Lizard with a powerful antibiotic and orders that she lie low and take care of herself. No doubt that would thrill Sandro to no end. Matteo could visualize him seething right now, and he gritted his teeth at the thought.

Matteo wondered if he could just keep the woman in this bedroom undetected and on the down low for a while. After all, she was staying in a different wing of the house from where Sandro lived. Although it hadn't worked so well when he tried to hide a litter of kittens, so he couldn't imagine why it would with a full-grown—and in all the right places—woman. Particularly one he suspected would become quite oppositional once she emerged from her febrile stupor, judging by her earlier hostile reactions.

Matteo had spent most of the day by her bedside. It seemed the polite thing to do. After all, if she woke from her fever-induced sleep in a strange place with no one at her side, it would likely frighten her. Although better to wake here in that state than to have done so in the toolshed.

It had been a long time since he simply did nothing. It was hard work sitting still. Well, he did have her to watch, which had its moments, so he wasn't entirely unoccupied. She was really quite beautiful now that she wasn't covered in mud and her long tawny hair was clean and shining. She was particularly attractive when her mouth was closed, with no contentious words coming out of it. That pleased him immensely. He could actually get used to watching her sleep. Or lapse in and out of consciousness, as it were.

She heaved a sigh and turned over, muttering something in her sleep he was unable to discern.

"What?" he said, standing to see if she needed something.

"You're sort of cute," she said. Or at least he thought she said that. He grinned. Nothing like sleep to serve as a truth serum. *Heh*. It felt a little bit like he was a voyeur eavesdropping on the demented mutterings of someone under the influence of a high fever. But she just said he was cute! And he couldn't help but have heard it, so it wasn't like it was an invasion of her privacy. Besides, she gave up that right when she trespassed on their property.

"If only you weren't such an asshole," she said. Or at least that's sure what it sounded like. He couldn't immediately think of any other word that rhymed with asshole that she might have said instead—passel, maybe? But really? No. Of course she wasn't talking about a passel of anything. Obviously she was talking about the real word, and he was going to have to stick with it.

So she thought he was an asshole. A cute asshole. He didn't know whether to take that as an insult or a compliment.

She tossed and turned a few more seconds, then started jabbering away again. "I've always loved Italian men. That hair. That smile. That chest. My hands would gladly wander over that chest."

Matteo's eyes opened wide. Was she pulling his leg? Was she actually awake and trying to make a mockery of him with all of this talk? He groaned, the idea of her hands roaming over him sounding better and better by the minute. The feeling there was mutual. He'd seen that rack on her, once she'd donned a T-shirt that morning. That still-damp and somewhat see-through T-shirt that revealed tight nipples and firm, beautiful breasts—they would fit his hands just right.

He thought about the purple panties and groaned some more. He shifted in his seat, making room for that tentpole that had suddenly materialized in his crotch. This would be a first: getting a hard-on thanks to a sick woman saying crazy things in her sleep. Clearly he hadn't been laid in awhile if this is what was getting him all hot and bothered.

Speaking of hot and bothered, he reached out his arm and placed his hand once again on her forehead. It no longer felt like a sizzling hot skillet at least. But she still felt pretty warm. He pulled her blanket up higher, tucking it beneath her to keep any chill air from reaching her body. Ironic, him tucking the blanket around her when his instincts were telling him to rip it off, if for no other reason than to get a good glimpse of what was beneath it. The thing is, he already knew—just enough so that possessing such information could be dangerous. He could get lost in her gorgeous set of tits, her narrow waist that flared to just-right grab-able hips, and her long lean legs that would wrap quite nicely around him if the situation ever presented itself. Which it wouldn't, fortunately or unfortunately.

After all, she'd been trying to leave when she passed

out. And he already said that's what he wanted her to do. Not to mention the problem with Sandro, who would more than likely drag her out of bed and put her on the next bus leaving Chianti by dinnertime. The good news was, for now Sandro would be distracted, holed up in his office trying to figure out precisely when the harvest would begin. Of course, then it would be all hands on deck, and Matteo, too, would be enlisted to do his fair share.

In the meantime, he was rather enjoying the solitude of watching Lizard sleep.

Lizzie had the unnerving sensation that someone was staring at her. And after her experience with that horrid farmer—God, was that another lifetime ago? Or was it just yesterday?—that was not a feeling she relished. But the weight of fatigue, her limbs pressed by gravity to the bed, her head quicksand heavy, was so powerful she couldn't muster up the energy to open her eyes to even see if she was actually back at Fattoria Luigi, about to be victimized by that vile man. The best she could do was muster up some sort of tepid objection to the man.

"Stop!" she said—or at least thought she had. "Leave me alone, you bastard. Get out of my bed!" She flailed her arms. Or maybe she did. In her head she certainly did, using all the strength she could generate to defend herself.

Whatever she'd just said or done, she'd apparently expended enough energy that she was unable to do much more than sleep for a while longer. She had no sense of how much time had elapsed or really where she was. Each time she half wondered it, she rolled back over and went to sleep. And in her restless slumber, she dreamed of a gorgeous dark-haired man who appeared astride a majestic white Arabian horse.

Normally she wasn't one to settle for cliché rescue fantasies, but it was her dreams, over which she had no control, so she went with it. The man looked a bit like the hottest star on Broadway, Lin-Manuel Miranda, from the show *Hamilton*. He'd been her fantasy man for the past year, after she saw a YouTube video of him, minus that facial hair. She was a fan of clean-shaven men. So if that banging piece of man-meat wanted to hop on a white steed and save her from herself, well, who was she to object to that? But was he saving her from herself? And if so, why would she need that? She was doing just fine on her own. Always had, always would.

She rolled over and thought more about the handsome man on the horse. She was a strong woman, always followed her instincts, proud to be fiercely independent. So why did the idea of a man carrying her off and caring for her sound so darned appealing? She didn't know the answer to that but she was too tired to worry about it.

"Fine. I surrender," she finally said before drifting back to a troubled sleep. "Take me, I'm yours."

Chapter Eight

GOOD Lord, this woman was a hot mess. Matteo worried what was at the root of her sleep-talking. Was she hallucinating? Or had something happened to her? She yelled at him to get out of her bed. But he'd taken plenty of precautions to respect her privacy from the minute he knew he had to help her in her desperation.

He even asked Allegra to help clean the poor thing up. Of course, Matteo could have simply put her to bed dirty in her damp clothes, but he couldn't imagine she'd want to be so sick in bed and covered in mud, so he asked if Allegra could give her a bath. Surely she couldn't be upset about that? Allegra was as kind and gentle as a grandmother. He discounted that immediately.

So who was this bastard she was screaming at—she truly yelled as if her life had depended on it—to get out of her bed? Something happened, somewhere, with someone. She was swinging her arms while she practically fought off whoever the culprit was. This couldn't just be fever-induced delirium, could it? But then after all of that rage, she said she surrendered. He had to admit when she said "Take me, I'm yours," it lit a candle of hope somewhere inside him. Weird, of course. After all, they were complete strangers.

His patient groaned and rolled over again, throwing the covers off, leaving Matteo no choice but to steal a glance at Lizard in his sister Valentina's pajamas. And just as soon as he could erase that his sister wore skimpy pajamas like this from his mind, he was going to marvel at the beautiful woman before him in the pale pink silky barely there pajamas. He made a note to find out the designer and send a quick thank-you note for his or her masterful skills. Because damn, the slinky camisole left little to the imagination; ditto for the tiny matching shorts.

Matteo gave himself a mental rebuke, trying hard to remember he was ogling a very sick woman, and that seemed inappropriate behavior. But she looked so hot. Even though physically, he knew she was, quite literally, hot. Which reminded him, he needed to wake her to take her medicine. And that scared him because he had a sneaking suspicion he would become the object of her ire. And he'd so enjoyed the quietude. But if he was ever going to get her better and out of here before Sandro got wind of her presence, he needed to be sure she took those pills.

He leaned forward to wake her but wasn't quite sure where it was safe to touch her. As she lay there, he noticed a lot of exposed flesh and it felt wrong to place his hands on any of that. But then again, what was covered, well, it was definitely not going to be okay to touch her there—it was, after all, covered for a reason. He couldn't push her head to wake her—that seemed to be antisocial behavior as well. He settled for a single finger on her very soft shoulder.

"Lizard," he said, his head near to her head. Which meant his eyes were that much closer to her body and those currently quite-unencumbered breasts. Jesus, he needed to take a cold shower, pronto. "Lizard. I'm sorry to wake you but you need to take your antibiotic now."

He gently pressed her shoulder with his pointer finger,

not daring to have any more contact with her. At the very least he didn't want her to coldcock him the minute she became conscious, what with her earlier utterings warning whoever was in her bed. Plus, that crack about his nuts, back in the shed. Obviously she was a force to be reckoned with, and he'd take no chances, thanks.

Her eyes fluttered open, and she squinted at Matteo, a look of confusion on her face.

"Hamilton?" she said to him.

He cocked his head. So was this Hamilton man the one who had been in her bed against her wishes? He wanted nothing more than to get to the bottom of this so he could find that Hamilton person and set him straight.

"Don't worry, Lizard. Hamilton is nowhere to be found. This is Matteo. We're taking good care of you now."

"But... Lin."

The plot thickened. Who was this woman, Lynn, he wondered? But alas, this was no time to press her on these matters.

"You're safe here," he said. "But you're quite sick. The doctor said you have pneumonia and it's very important for you to take your medicine now so that you can get better. And if you want me to get hold of your friend Lynn just let me know how to reach her."

He tried to motion for her to sit up a bit, so he could help her with a cup of water to swallow the pill. But she didn't have the energy to do so on her own, leaving him to assist as discreetly as possible. While placing his hand behind her and another around her stomach, he helped her to shift but not before his arm grazed her tight belly. He bent over awkwardly to be sure his crotch didn't press against her and tried to avoid betraying his overactive libido's reaction to that accidentally copped feel. He must have looked ridiculous, crooked over, trying to hoist her at an odd angle like that.

Finally he positioned her upright enough so that he could he reach for a pill.

"Open wide," he said.

She opened her mouth slightly, which would have to do. He slipped the pill onto her tongue, such an intimate act to do with someone he didn't even know. He held the glass of water to her mouth and tipped it toward her as she swallowed. He honestly didn't spill that drip across her chest on purpose, but the way it turned the silky fabric almost see-through across one nipple was without a doubt an added bonus. He went to dab it, only to realize that would be a bad idea, so he let it be.

"Sorry about that," he said, pointing at her breast, which only made things more awkward. "Um, is there anything I can do for you, Lizard?"

She frowned and started to talk but stopped, wincing against it. Instead she shook her head and slumped back down to sleep some more.

There were a lot of confusing things Lizzie wanted to understand. For instance, what was up with this guy with the friendly eyes who could be an understudy for Lin-Manuel Miranda, he looked so much like him. God, he was so hot. Unless she was hallucinating and he didn't actually take her breath away. Though maybe that was the infection she was fighting that was taking her breath away. She couldn't believe she felt like such crap yet still had the capacity to objectify this guy for his sex appeal. Obviously humanity was doomed if this was the case. Aside from the *Hamilton* doppelganger mystery, she also wouldn't have minded knowing why he kept calling her Lizard.

But for now, her throat hurt like a son of a bitch and it felt like her lungs were contained in a pressure chamber, it ached so much to breathe. She didn't want to expend the energy nor fight through the pain to communicate with the man. She wasn't even sure who he was or why he was helping her. All she knew was she was snuggled up in an incredibly comfortable bed and at this point, that's all that mattered. With any luck, she might find her way back to that dream with the man on the white horse.

Chapter Nine

LIZZIE woke with a start, completely disoriented and wondering where she was. Wherever it was, the room was pitch black, and as she reached her arm across the bed, there was no sign of another person sharing it with her. Which was a relief and a disappointment. A bed like this was meant to be shared. Although with whom, well, that was another question. Nevertheless, she knew she wasn't alone as she heard the soft snuffle of a sleeping person.

She closed her eyes and she was back at that horrible shack with Luigi pressing himself against her, and she gasped as it all came flooding back: hitting Luigi with her elbow, racing from the property as if her life depended on it—and perhaps it did. She'd never know, thank God.

Then all the walking and the rain and at long last finding the shelter. And then that man arriving at dawn, waking her from her broken slumber. Was that the same man who gave her the medicine... which she simply took without asking questions? God, she was so losing her edge if she did that. As a woman traveling alone for so long, she knew better than to just take something someone gave her, be it a pill or food or drink.

That man—was he the one in her room right now? And if so, where was he? She rubbed the sleep from her eyes and sat up a bit, scanning the room until her gaze settled on her Lin-Manuel lookalike, curled up on a sofa, softly snoring. Well. This was interesting. Was he guarding her so she didn't do something he didn't want her to do? Or was he watching over her (sound asleep, natch) to make sure she was all right? And setting that all aside for a minute, boy did she have to pee. She shifted and resolved to get out of bed and find the bathroom, which couldn't be far.

Her hand fumbled on the nightstand next to the bed till she found a lamp. She pulled the cord and flooded the room with soft light. She didn't want to wake that man up, but she needed to see her way in this unfamiliar room. A nearby clock showed it was going on three in the morning. How long had she been asleep? She tried to piece together events from the past day. She remembered being in the shed and then that man showed up. Was that him? On the sofa? Why had she not noticed his looks before? Maybe because he was busy being a jerk to her, that's why. But then what happened? The last thing she remembered was hoisting her large pack on her back. And then what?

She wasn't feeling particularly steady on her feet but nature called. She fumbled her way across the bedroom, holding on to the footboard of the huge king-size bed she'd been occupying. She looked down at her pajamas and wondered where the heck they'd come from.

"Stop right now!" she heard a man's voice say as she about jumped out of her skin.

She gasped. "What?"

Before she could say anything else he was up and right there, grabbing her arm, helping to usher her safely to the bathroom. He was lucky she was too weak to use any of the personal defense skills she'd learned back in college, or he'd have had a knee to the crotch and two fingers in his eyeballs by now.

"I'm sorry, I hadn't thought about how you'd get to the bathroom if need be," he said. "I tried to think of everything else. In the meantime, I must have dozed off."

She looked at him as he rubbed his hand over his sleep-worn face. Even a mask of fatigue didn't diminish his handsome good looks. How was it possible she hadn't noticed that before? Maybe she was still so shaken from the Luigi episode. Maybe it was because she had been standing there shivering, naked, with nothing but a drop cloth. Or maybe it was his accusatory tone that rubbed her the wrong way and kept her from even registering anything else about him but for his jerkiness. If that was even a word.

"Um, I'm perfectly capable of finding the bathroom on my own, thanks," she said. It was all coming back to her: how she had to let her guard down and how exposed and vulnerable she felt when she had to rely on other people to help her. It was so not in her repertoire. She needed to put a stop to that right now.

"Are you kidding? You were planted on the cement floor of the toolshed this morning, out cold," he said. "I'm not going to let you walk yourself to the bathroom or anywhere, for that matter."

She glared at him. "I'm sorry, but who died and made you my caretaker?"

She tried to shrug off his supportive hand on her elbow but he wouldn't let her.

He stopped when they got to the entrance to the bathroom. "Wow, you don't make it easy for people to be kind to you, do you?"

She pursed her lips and pondered his comment. Actually, no, she didn't. Because she knew that in this world, you had to fend for yourself, and if you had to rely

53

on others, you might find yourself hurt down the road. She'd learned that the hard way.

"Look," she said, gazing down at the floor while she traced imaginary images with her toe on the terra-cotta tile flooring. "I'm sorry if I'm a bit brusque. I'm not used to dealing with people. And I'm really not used to have anyone tell me what I can and can't do."

He cocked his head. "What do you mean you're not used to dealing with people?"

"Uh, can we continue this in a minute?" she said, crossing her legs as she pointed to the bathroom door.

He thumped his forehead with the palm of his hand. "Of course." His face reddened. "But, uh, do you need some help in there? I don't want you to fall and hit your head."

She rolled her eyes and went into the room, shutting the door behind her and locking it tight.

Apparently the medicine was working. Gone was the needy, sick woman, and in her stead Matteo found the defensive, stubborn, cantankerous one impossibly appealing despite those traits. He must have some serious streak of self-loathing to find that attractive. He wondered why; it's not as if his mother beat him or anything. Nope, he grew up perfectly happy. Maybe his older brother gave him far too much shit. But nothing that would require therapy for being turned on by a tetchy woman who didn't appreciate that he'd helped her when she was at her lowest.

After she came back out, Matteo decided to take a chance and press the issue with her.

"So, Lizard," he said.

"Why do you keep saying that to me?" she said. "Because if this is some pet name, you need to stop it."

He squinted at her, wondering what the ever-loving hell she was talking about. "You mean 'Lizard'?"

She shook her head. "Yes. Why are you saying 'lizard' to me?"

"Because it's your name."

"What?"

She gave him one of those "are you dense?" looks that made him super annoyed.

"When you passed out on the ground, and I was trying to revive you—"

"Ohmigod, I remember that now. You slapped me!"

"I wouldn't call it a slap. I'd say it was more of trying to wake you up. I was worried you were going to die."

She laughed. "When was the last time a hard slap woke up a dead person?"

"You got me there." He grinned. "But I didn't know what to do. I've never had someone pass out on me before—"

"Oh God, I didn't pass out *on* you did I?"

"I should tell you yes, just so you'd be embarrassed or something other than angry at me. But no, you didn't pass out on me. But rather on my watch. And then after you came to, I tried to find out your name and you told me it was Lizard."

Lizzie let out a laugh. "Oh, that is so perfect. Lizard. Me! Lizard," she said. "No, my name is decidedly not 'lizard.' I'm Lizzie. Lizzie Moretti."

She reached out her hand to shake his.

"Matteo Romeo," he said.

"Really?" she said. "Where's Juliet?"

He rolled his eyes. "There's one I've yet to hear."

She shrugged. "Yeah, I guess with the name Romeo and all," she said. "But it beats 'Lizard.'"

Matteo figured she was warmed up enough and maybe she wouldn't bite his head off if he got too personal, so he decided to ask what he was dying to know.

"You said you're not used to dealing with people," he said as he grabbed her arm, trying to steer her back to the bed, but she swatted his arm away. She was one tough customer.

"I live my life, that's all," she said. "I don't have to worry about people and no one has to worry about me. I come and go as I please and I make a point of not getting too comfortable in one place."

"I'm sorry," he said. "That sounds sort of lonely."

"Hey, I'm a realist," she said. "All good things must come to an end. So I'm just ready for it that way. No surprises, no heartache, no loss. If you don't rely on others, you don't have to learn to live without them."

This was a foreign concept for Matteo, being one of seven kids. Everyone bugged each other, everyone leaned on each other, everyone told each other what to do and when to do it. But they loved each other and they were there for each other in the hard times, like when his father died. They cried together and blamed each other together and shunned each other together, all as they grieved the loss of a man who was so important in their lives.

But even when they were apart—even when Matteo left to go figure himself out—still his family loomed large over him. Always WWTRD was in the back of his head: What Would The Romeos Do? He could no sooner escape his family than change his blood type from O positive.

"So why did you choose to live such an isolated life?"

She'd climbed back into bed. "That kind of took it out of me," she said, referring to the long stroll to the bathroom. "Maybe another time?"

Matteo heaved a sigh. This woman was quite the mystery. A puzzle with so many missing pieces. And he had all the time in the world to piece them together. The question was: how long was she going to stick around to let him?

Chapter Ten

LIZZIE hadn't slept this much since, well, ever. She was wide awake well before dawn with nothing to do and unfortunately had as little energy as those three-toed sloths she used to see hanging from the trees in Costa Rica when she worked on a farm there. Which meant she was just there, alone with her thoughts, with absolutely nothing to do.

Being stuck in bed sick reminded her of happier childhood days when everything was so much better in her life, and even being sick took on the veneer of pleasantness upon reflection. Her mother would set her up with ginger ale and saltine crackers and chicken noodle soup that came in a packet—the kind you added hot water to—and she could watch television to her heart's content, cuddled up with the cat on the sofa till she felt all better. Funny how something as lousy as being ill could seem so romanticized now. She must have been in a state of fever-induced hallucination.

She sighed as she glanced around the dim room. Not a television in sight. And no energy in her weakened body to get up and go in search of one. Although she still wasn't quite sure what her status was with this Matteo Romeo guy and whether she should even leave the confines of this room. She'd obviously been caught trespassing on the man's property. And he'd seemed ready to haul her off to the cops for it. But then he changed his tune and helped her out and set her up in a bedroom that could put the Ritz to shame: heavenly bedding with a fat, feathered duvet and one of those padded mattresses that you sink into while heaving a sigh of joy bordering on downright orgasmic.

There looked to be artwork on the walls. Artwork! Who has that? If she had a room—which she didn't, because even the family home was gone now, and her mother and her husband sure didn't keep a room set up for her in their tiny rambler in that decrepit East Texas town they lived in—she'd probably still have posters on the wall, like the tacky ones you might put on your dorm wall. Maybe something aspirational, like the picture of a beautiful mansion she might want to live in someday. Nah. More likely she'd hang something with a smart-ass phrase that fit her worldview, like: You've Probably Mistaken me for Someone Who Cares. But definitely not paintings that looked like they were plucked from the walls of a museum.

Whoever this Matteo Romeo was, he apparently had some family money. No wonder he wanted her out of here. From what she could tell, rich people didn't want to share the wealth with the other half. Make that 99 percent. Which was fine by her. What she lacked in money she made up for in life experiences, and she didn't need a ton of financial resources to work her way around the world and live her life to the fullest.

Though even she had to admit, the events of this week were a low point for her. But hey, hitting the nadir of her nomadic life meant it was easier to calibrate the good times as such. You can't have highs without the lows. She'd survived the episode (so far), and it only contributed to making her a stronger woman. Admittedly, it was lucky for her Matteo Romeo had a bit of a soft spot for women who passed out in his toolshed. She could have been left lying in a pool of blood and died from pneumonia.

Now you're being a little melodramatic, she thought. But if she were to be honest with herself, she'd admit that she missed having someone to care for her. Having attachments with other humans sometimes seemed to be burdensome, but then again, having attachments with other humans was also sort of what life was all about. Maybe she was giving the whole notion short shrift by detaching as she had.

Her stomach rumbled. *God, food would be good.* Though swallowing anything right now sounded downright torturous. She wished she did have a bowl of that sodium-laden soup mix—at least she knew she could swallow that without doubling over in pain.

Her protector—or was he her jailor? She'd yet to discern that—stirred. He was asleep again on the sofa, and she hadn't wanted to wake him because, well, the whole thing was rather awkward. She couldn't help but notice how he'd assessed her last night when she walked to the bathroom in just the pajamas she had on. She could hardly blame him, though; the things didn't leave much to the imagination. But still, it just seemed awkward. She, the unwanted intruder-turned-houseguest, he, the peevish lord of the manor, or whatever he was, protecting his birthright from the likes of her.

"Good morning, Lizard." His voice disrupted her thoughts. He had a soothing voice, actually. A warm, comforting timbre, like a cup of hot tea on a cold day.

"You startled me."

"The feeling's mutual," he said. "You going down like a KO'd boxer yesterday took me equally by surprise."

"I'm sorry for the inconvenience," she said.

He shook his head as he walked toward her. His hair was mussed up, and his eyes were puffy with sleep. Still he looked impossibly handsome, which was so not what Lizzie wanted to think about the man.

"I couldn't exactly leave you to your own devices back there, now could I?"

"I'm sure I'd have been fine."

"You are a fiercely independent one, aren't you?"

"Is there something wrong with that?"

He shrugged. "Probably not. But there's nothing wrong with needing help every now and then. And by the looks of you, I'd say you needed help."

"Thanks for that."

"By thanks, are you thanking me for helping or being sarcastic because I said you needed help?"

"You want the truth?"

"Somehow I think you'd speak it regardless," he said. He reached for her glass of water and the bottle of pills on the nightstand. "Ready for another dose?"

She looked at the bottle, the label written in Italian, of course. She was in Italy, so why wouldn't it be? "How do I know you're not giving me some bad drug that will knock me out and kill me?"

He laughed. "So a hardened, independent, sarcastic cynic with a vivid imagination. Adding to the list. Any other personality traits you'd like to own up to?"

She glared at him. "Mistrustful."

"That goes without saying, I would think." He opened the bottle and took out a pill. "Time for medicine roulette, then. Is Matteo giving his sick houseguest essential medicine to make her better, or is he slowly killing her with

61

some deadly poison so that he's left with a dead body that he has to dispose of? And if so, why wouldn't he have just left her to die in the toolshed? You decide."

He waved the pill in front of her face and laughed a fake maniacal laugh.

She rolled her eyes. "Fine, if you put it that way." She grabbed the pill and the water and downed her medicine. "But I'm holding out judgment on your ulterior motives."

He arched a brow. "My ulterior motives are to make sure that you and my brother don't cross paths, because, well, if you think I'm bad, wait till you meet Alessandro. His idea of kindness might be using the thumb screws on you until you confess your crimes to him."

"In that case, my thumbs are in trouble because I've got no crimes to own up to."

He tipped his head, doubting her. "Well… breaking and entering could be for starters."

Her eyes opened wide in disbelief. "I didn't break anything! Yes, I entered but the door was open. Well, it was unlocked. Besides, what would you have done if you were me?"

"That's hard to say, Lizard, since I don't know anything about your circumstances, except what I encountered, which was a bunch of wet panties, a bra or two, and a nearly naked you clothed only in a farm tarp."

Lizzie blushed and opted to stonewall instead of confessing. "Did I tell you already to stop calling me Lizard?"

Always safest to keep your cards close at hand.

Chapter Eleven

MATTEO was learning quickly that Lizzie would have made an excellent prisoner of war. Which works well when you're a prisoner of war, but is actually a huge pain in the ass when someone is just trying to be nice to you. Yet for some weird reason, this made him just want to double down to figure out what would ultimately break down the veritable fortress (complete with moat and crocodiles and probably vats of boiling oil to pour down on interlopers) she protected herself with.

Sort of ironic that here she was an indignant intruder on his family property, yet she shunned intruders in her personal life, space, and world. It was making him nuts. And Matteo loved nothing better than to try to get to the bottom of a vexing problem. It's why he loved math so much in school. And why he was the one his father always sent out to the fields to figure out where the wild boar were breaking into the property, as well as the other animals that loved to feast on the grapes in the fields.

Little Matteo performed his detective work like a professional, and invariably found the source and solved the problem. Grown-up Matteo crossed his arms and gazed at Lizzie, realizing she wasn't much different than a wild boar—sort of surly and demanding, protesting loudly, and yet perfectly happy to squat on his land.

Too bad he couldn't turn *her* into a nice pappardelle a ragù di cinghiale like he would with an obstinate wild boar…

Matteo felt a little grungy after having slept on the sofa overnight, and he wanted nothing more than to brush his teeth and take a shower. But now with his houseguest for the foreseeable future—at least until Doctor Sarducci cleared her medically—he needed to figure out what to do with her.

"You must be starving," he said. "Is there something that sounds good to eat?"

Lizzie pursed her lips in thought. "I feel like I haven't eaten in days," she said. "Of course I basically haven't, no thanks to Luigi."

Luigi, he thought. *Another one I need to figure out regarding his role in all this. Right after I find that Hamilton guy. And her friend Lynn.*

That Lizzie was gonna be a tough code to crack, but he wasn't going to stop until he could find out what that American man, Hamilton—with a name like that he must be American—did to her.

"I suppose if I asked what that meant you'd not bother to tell me anyhow?"

She shook her head. "My life is a closed book, I'm afraid."

"In which case, I guess I should try to scratch up some food for you in the kitchen?"

"You're going to cook for me?"

He laughed and shook his head. "Heavens no. Hopefully Allegra is in there already and I'll see what she can make."

"But my throat hurts desperately." She rubbed along the column of her neck. "I can't think of anything that would go down easily."

Matteo squinted his eyes. He could definitely think of something that would go down easily. But that, too, wasn't going to happen, so he'd better remove his mind from the gutter once again.

"Let me talk to Allegra and see what she can come up with."

"While you're at it, do you think she can cook up a television set? Nothing personal but I'm sort of bored."

Matteo shrugged. "Americans and their television. The rest will do you good. Why don't you go back to sleep and I'll be back in a little while with some food for you?"

Lizzie closed her eyes but sleep refused to come. She tossed and turned for a while and eventually gave up, only to stare at the ceiling, which she realized for the first time had a fresco painted on it depicting angels and scenes of war and bible stories. This was definitely the first bedroom she'd ever encountered with a frescoed ceiling. At least she could spend some time staring at that when she grew bored.

After counting the number of men with ripped abs in the ceiling for several minutes, she grew impatient. She climbed out of bed and walked to the bathroom, bringing along her water glass to refill it. When she got there, she noticed for the first time the huge bathtub that took up a third of the room. How had she forgotten about that thing? She had a very vague recollection of Allegra, the family maid or whatever she was, helping her to undress and step into the warm tub.

A warm bath sounded just about perfect, so she inserted the drain stopper and turned on the water, letting the tub fill with piping-hot water as she poured some divine-smelling bath oil in. What an indulgence, two baths in the space of a day. For a woman who hadn't had the benefit of a private bathroom in a couple of years, she could get quickly used to living the pampered life. While the tub filled, she explored the rest of the bathroom and noticed a brand-new toothbrush had been left on the sink along with a tube of toothpaste. *How considerate*, she thought. *When he's not being accusatory he can be awfully thoughtful.*

She brushed her teeth and rinsed and even gargled with warm water, which felt sort of good on her throat. She couldn't believe how she'd gone from cold and wet to debilitated to approaching human in such a relatively short period of time. As much as she didn't want to admit it, she was awfully grateful that Matteo had come to her rescue.

She tried for a minute to imagine herself weak and sick, lugging her backpack for who-knows-how-many-miles until she could find somewhere to go. Plus, she wouldn't have gone to a doctor and probably would have died alone in the forest, only to be eaten by wild boars. Again with the imagination.

Lizzie shrugged off the cami and bottoms, hanging them on the door hook, then slipped into the hot tub.

This is as close to heaven as I will ever get while still being alive, she thought. *And maybe even once I'm dead. But I'm going to enjoy this while I can because the road is going to look cold and lonely after this little diversion.*

As she leaned against the back of the tub, she had

some random thoughts: how cute Matteo looked when he woke up, all sleepy-eyed yet concerned. How much he looked like Lin-Manuel Miranda, but she could never tell him that. Besides, he wouldn't know who that was.

She closed her eyes and thought about the actor. *Who actually looks good in colonial clothes?* But damn, that man looked hawt in them. Even his facial hair worked. Though she much preferred the earlier versions of him without it. She wondered what Matteo would look like dressed up in those foppish clothes and decided he looked much better in his tight blue jeans and black cashmere V-neck. No doubt this was dressing down for him. Italian men, with the exception of the loutish Luigi, were usually quite stylish.

Her eyelids were so heavy and the warmth and the steam so enveloping, it was easy to drift off to sleep…

Chapter Twelve

MATTEO returned a little while later with a plate of pasta al pomodoro. What better filling food was there to slide down your sore throat than noodles with a light tomato sauce?

After turning the knob and opening the door with his hip, he stepped into the room to set Lizzie up for her meal.

"I think you'll find this dish satisfactory," he said as he looked toward the bed, only to find it empty. "Lizzie? Lizard?" He looked around the whole room, worried she'd fallen, but she was nowhere to be found. The bathroom door was open, so surely she wasn't in there or she'd have closed it. "Lizzie?" he said, to no response.

He walked into the bathroom to find her in the tub, her mouth level with the water.

"Lizzie!" he shouted, rushing over to save her.

"Ahhhh!" she shouted as she started from her sleep, terrified.

"You almost drowned!" he said, reaching to help her out of the tub.

"I did no such thing!" she said, closing her arms over her exposed breasts and crossing her legs.

"Your head was about to submerge," he said. "You can't just do that. You nearly gave me a heart attack! Think how I'd have felt if I found you, drowned in my bathtub, on my watch."

"You and your watch," she said. "I had everything

under control. I was not anywhere near death, I assure you."

Matteo looked down at her. The water, which had been disturbed in the frenzy just a minute ago, had settled down to a calm state. Calm and clear, so that he could see most of Lizzie's naked body, which took his breath away. She was beautiful. And naked. And so very off-limits, it wasn't even funny.

"Well," he said, wiping his wet hands on his jeans, trying to also discreetly tamp down the burgeoning hard-on he could do nothing about, dammit. "Um, please do me a favor and don't scare me like that again. I could have asked Allegra to help you."

"I am fine," she said. "I don't need help to bathe. I'm a big girl."

Big in all the right places, he thought.

"That you are," he said, scrunching his nose. "So, uh, I'll leave you to eat your meal. Would you rather it in the bathtub? Or in bed?"

If it was up to him, he'd rather have her first in the bathtub and then in the bed. He had to remind himself that wasn't the point of her being here nor of him helping her out. Rather he was being a good Samaritan and she the Samaritee—or whatever that would be called—even though she was actually pretty terrible at it, what with her ongoing refusal to let anyone help her.

"Thanks," she said. "I'll dry off and eat it in bed. If you can just let me know the next time I'm due for a pill, you won't have to bother me at all."

"It's no bother, really it's not."

She frowned, which he took to mean it was a bother for her.

"Fine," he said. "I'll leave you to your own self-destruction if you'd rather. Let me know if I need to send the coroner in for you, please."

Before leaving the room, he took one last peek at her, because, well, naked. What sort of man would he be if he didn't leave himself with a parting image of that beautiful, bare creature?

Well, that was awkward, she thought as she toweled off. And awfully rude of him to bust in on her in the bathtub. Doesn't anyone ever knock?

Even more awkward was when she truly got a look at him as he stood there, agog. As if he'd never encountered a naked woman before.

Luckily Lizzie was plenty used to strange men happening upon her in various states of undress; that tended to be how it was when you shared cramped quarters and communal bathrooms with fellow travelers. The funny thing about Matteo, though, is that he seemed to be almost in awe of her, something she'd never encountered before with a man. She caught him staring at her, and her eyes met his brown ones—so close she could see flecks of copper and silver twinkling in them, like some prehistoric minerals preserved in amber, reflecting the glint of the sun coming in through the window.

The man was undoubtedly handsome. In an alternate universe, well, he would certainly be easy on the eyes. If her eyes were looking for something easy. As it was, she was itching to get a move on, and just as soon as her energy was back, she'd be out of here. Though she'd miss that comfy bed.

She dressed and returned to the bedroom, where she found a tray with a bowl of pasta and a vase with one baby-sized sunflower in it to cheer her up. Dammit, the man was making it hard for her to remain detached and disinterested.

Matteo was talking with his sister Valentina and his mother over breakfast, getting them up to speed on their houseguest. His sister knew about Lizzie because of the loaner pajamas and his mother because of the "loaning" of Allegra. He trusted them both to keep this information from Sandro.

"So you were calling her a *lucertola*?" his sister said with a laugh, shaking her head. "I'm sure she really appreciated you calling her a scaly-skinned reptile, Matteo."

"It was an honest mistake," he said. "Anyone could have made it."

"*Mio figlio*," his mamma said. "My son. This is so like you, bringing in a stray. It's what you did as a child. Whether it was kittens or dogs or hedgehogs. You were always finding wayward creatures and giving them a place to sleep." She scrubbed his hair. "You're a good boy."

"Mamma, I think he has ulterior motives with this one," Valentina said. "Allegra told me she's quite beautiful. Or at least once she got all the mud off of her." She elbowed her brother in the ribs.

His eyes grew wide. "Trust me, this had nothing to do with her looks. I was fully prepared to turn her away onto the streets—she was sleeping in our toolshed, with the harvest looming. No way was I going to be responsible for that."

"Yet here you are, responsible for that," Valentina said.

"I couldn't just leave her there, passed out on the floor. What kind of monster would I be?"

His sister pressed her forehead to his. "You're the least monster-ish person I know, Matteo. Like Mamma said, you're a good boy. And I know you're just trying to help this poor woman."

"Thank you for your vote of confidence," he said. "Now how can we keep this from Alessandro before he goes *pazzo* on me?"

"Your brother Sandro is a reasonable man," his mother said. "He won't go crazy on you. Besides, he's so distracted with Taylor, he doesn't have time to go sniffing all over the house for strange and unexpected houseguests."

"I hope you're right about that," Matteo said. "Hell hath no fury like Sandro when he's pissed off."

"Sometimes Sandro gets a little possessive of the Romeo name," his mother said. "But he means well. Don't forget, he took on much of the burden of the business when Papà died. He feels vested in its success. He carries the weight of many generations of Romeos on his shoulders."

"Yeah, yeah, yeah," Matteo said. "But he doesn't have to be such a dick about it."

"Bite your tongue," his mother said, pretending to slap him. "No badmouthing each other around here. We're all family, and family sticks together."

Matteo made his hands into a puppet and mocked his mother for repeating something she'd said to them daily since they were small children.

She wagged her finger at him as Valentina took a quick swig of her espresso.

"Well, I don't know about you, Mamma, but I can't wait to go meet her!" she stood and dusted crumbs off her lap.

"Mamma mia, Valentina, no. Please, just leave her alone," Matteo said. "You'll scare her away like a feral cat."

His sister made her hands into pretend cat claws. "Meow." She grinned. "It'll be fun. She'll totally fall for me. Everybody does."

Her brother rolled his eyes. It would be just fitting if Lizard fell for his sister instead of him. Not that he wanted her, but still.

Chapter Thirteen

"**KNOCK**, knock," a voice said from outside the bedroom door. "Room service! Coming in!"

Lizzie turned her head just in time to see a stunningly beautiful, tall, slender brunette with long, loose curls and warm brown eyes stroll into the room. She was dressed like a fashion model: form-fitting black leather pants, spiky leather ankle boots, a black leather biker jacket, with a creamy white scarf draped effortlessly around her neck. So perfectly Italian—and entirely opposite of Lizzie, who never once in her life put on a pair of high-heeled boots—or wore leather, for that matter.

She had something in a bowl in her left hand and gave a little wave with her right one.

"Hi!" she said, her smile bright and wide and sincere. "I'm Valentina—I'm the Romeo you'll fall in love with. And I brought you this."

She handed a bowl of chocolate gelato to Lizzie, who gazed up at her as if she'd just been visited by an angel. Ice cream... was this woman a mind reader or what?

She smiled back. "I'd actually sell my soul to the person who would bring me chocolate ice cream, so, yeah, count on me falling in love with you at the very least," Lizzie said, waving back. "I'm Lizzie by the way."

"Lizard?" Valentina said with a giggle.

Lizzie shook her head. "Exactly. That's me: Lizzie the Lizard. Note the spiny skin and moveable eyelids. If you're lucky I'll show you how I can catch a fly with my tongue." She gave her a wink.

"So you're on the mend, then?" Valentina said. "I say that because Allegra told me you were about half-dead yesterday. Thank goodness for miracle drugs, no?"

Lizzie nodded. "You said it. I hardly have a recollection of what happened yesterday, to tell the truth. I was so out of it. Though I have to say I've never had someone give me a bath before, so there was that."

Valentina knit her brows. "Not even with a guy? Oh, sweetie, you're so missing out."

Lizzie blushed. It was laughable how much she hadn't done with a guy but certainly never *that*. Maybe she was socially stunted but she'd only ever had a few awkward sexual encounters with boys when she was in college, and since then, she'd been on the move, never anywhere long enough to establish a relationship. She wasn't one to just sleep with (let alone bathe with!) anyone she'd just met. Nowadays when she had a chance to get cleaned up, it involved a lot of scrubbing much dirt off her skin. Nothing sexy about that. Working the land was not for anyone afraid to get dirt under their fingernails.

"I'll have to add it to my list," Lizzie said, feeling a bit embarrassed. "Though I probably don't have to worry about that any time in the near future. My lifestyle doesn't exactly lend itself to such things."

"I see." Valentina nodded. "Interesting... So what exactly is your lifestyle? And maybe you should expand your horizons so that your lifestyle does lend itself to 'such things.'" She made air quotes and laughed again. "Sorry, Matteo always yells at me because I'm so forward. But really, what's your deal?"

"My deal…" Lizzie said, rubbing her chin in thought. "I've been traveling. Well, working and traveling. I work to travel. And right now I'm in Italy, though it seems probable it won't be as long as I'd hoped."

"Why not? And what kind of work do you do?"

"Whatever I can do to have a roof over my head and some food in my stomach. I've mostly worked in agriculture, though I've done some other things as well, like doing prep work in the kitchen of a tiny beachside restaurant in Phuket, Thailand. And I learned how to weave rugs in a small village in Morocco. I wasn't very good at it, though. But mostly my 'specialty' is planting and harvesting."

Valentina reached over and squeezed Lizzie's exposed arm. "That explains these things," she said. "I have to admit to immediate bicep envy the minute I saw them. Those are some pretty nicely cut arms you've got. I guess it reflects the hard work you've been doing."

Lizzie blushed again. "Wow, I never thought twice about my arms. You think they look good? I just use them—I never gave them a second's consideration."

"Women would pay good money for those things," she said. "Without having to work for it, mind you."

"I don't mind hard work. Makes the day go faster, and you sleep like a baby."

"So why'd you choose this lifestyle?" Valentina said. "It sounds like you're some sort of migrant worker. Don't get me wrong, nothing against that. Just seems a hard way to live."

Lizzie frowned. Until now it was really quite ideal for her. But she'd been in good health and for the most part, she'd had relatively good experiences.

She was pretty spooked by what happened to her at the farm. She'd been going along thinking she was so perfectly safe, but that was an illusion, it seemed. Or maybe she'd been instantly spoiled by being plunged into this luxurious escape from her lifestyle, something she never dreamed of but had to admit was a pretty darned agreeable way to live.

"I'd finished university and wanted to see the world," she said. "But didn't have the money to see anything much past my hometown. I had no commitments, no reason to stick around, and every reason imaginable to go see that open world. So I did it. I saved enough money for a flight to Costa Rica, where I worked on a pineapple plantation for six months in the packaging plant." She frowned. "Great country, hate the fruit now. No more pineapples for me, sadly. Totally sick of them."

"Wow, that sounds so exotic!" Valentina said. "Then where'd you go?"

Lizzie started enumerating on her fingers. "Let's see. I've been to so many places, I lose track of some of them. I've been to Peru, Bolivia, Norway, France, Germany, Turkey, Morocco, the Democratic Republic of the Congo, Kenya, Thailand, Vietnam, Indonesia, Bangladesh, Fiji—"

"Wait, it sounds like you've been to the whole world already."

Lizzie laughed. "I've hardly skimmed the surface. So many places still to see."

"But how do you do it?"

"I usually stay someplace in exchange for room and board, and that means putting in about twenty hours of work there each week, which gives me time to work elsewhere to earn some extra money. I save that money so that when it's time to move on I have a way to get there. Sometimes I hitch rides, which isn't my first choice. I even hitched a ride on a freighter to cross an ocean. The good thing is that people are very kind." She stopped, thinking about what might have happened with Luigi had she not been immediately alert and he so drunk that she could get away in time. It made her shudder. "Usually."

"That sounds like you've had some bad experiences."

Lizzie frowned. "I'd rather not talk about them. Much nicer to focus on the good stuff."

"Fair enough," Valentina said. "I have to say I'm so impressed with your bravery. I could never do that, traveling alone and with so little money. Besides I'd never be able to lug a half dozen suitcases everywhere." She laughed. "How do you travel so light?"

"Everything I own I carry on my back," Lizzie said, looking around the room. "Which reminds me, my pack. I have no idea where it is. It has my whole life in it."

"I'm sure it's fine," Valentina said. "Knowing Matteo he sent it off to be dry-cleaned and stitched up if there were any holes in it."

"Ugh, I hope no one's been near it. It probably reeks to the high heavens," she said. "The thing was rained on for a couple of hours. I hate to think of how awful everything must smell inside my pack."

"Let me do some investigative work on it and I'll let you know. In the meantime, get some sleep, Lizzie the Lizard," Valentina said. "And by the way, my pajamas suit you! Consider them yours."

"Oh, no, please, I can't accept your gift. But thank you for lending them to me. They're amazingly soft. They make me feel elegant, like royalty."

"Perfect, since the Romeo family harkens back to the earliest days of Italian royalty. And just FYI, you have no choice in the matter. I won't take no for an answer. Now I've got to be off to get my nails done. Ciao, bella!" She blew her an air kiss and slipped out the door just as she'd slipped in, leaving Lizzie to wonder what weather system had just blown into the room. Whatever it was, the breeze felt good. Really good. As in she could get used to this.

Chapter Fourteen

"**GEEZ**, Val, you're in there twenty minutes and you extracted more information from the woman than I have in days—or what seems like days."

Valentina brushed her nails on her jacket as if she was a pro at this. "What can I say? I'm like a human truth serum. You're welcome!"

"Right, thanks for at least finding out something for me," he said. "I think we're going to have to play this good cop-bad cop act with her if we're ever going to know all that we need to know about her."

"Why do you need to know her life story?" Valentina said. "If I didn't know better, I'd suspect you had a crush on her. My brother's in *lurv*." She pinched his cheek and he swatted her away.

"Stop," he said. "I'm just curious. And I think I'm entitled to be. I've spent enough time with the woman, and I did save her from whatever might have happened to her. Surely I deserve a little background story on her for my efforts."

"What does Mamma always say to us?"

"Good things come to those who wait?"

"Yeah, that too. But I was thinking 'in due time.'"

"But due time might not come before she slips out the back door. I just know the minute she's up for it, she'll be gone. At least she can't go until she finds her pack."

"Wait a minute—you hid it from her?"

He blushed. "Not exactly."

"What do you mean not exactly? Either you did or you didn't. There's no middle ground there."

"I didn't hide the thing. I just left it in the toolshed. I didn't know what else to do with it and I was sort of busy lugging her back at the time. I could only carry so much dead weight. I actually hadn't thought again about it till now."

"Well, crap," his sister said. "She was asking about it. And worried that everything was going to smell musty because it was so wet."

"It sure seemed wet yesterday."

"Then we need to find that thing and do something with it," she said. "We can take it and all of her stuff to get cleaned. I'm sure Allegra would help out. She's good at making everything smell delicious."

"They're clothes, not food, V. I don't think delicious has anything to do with it."

Valentina waved her hand. "You are such a guy. Of course it matters. Who doesn't love something smelling delicious? Every girl worth her salt does."

"Have you had a look at her? She's not exactly the girliest of girls."

"It's adorable, isn't it?" Valentina said. "I'd love to get my hands on her for a day or two and introduce her to the world of girlie things. I'd have her converted in no time at all. And it sounds like she needs it. Can you believe, she's never taken a bath with a guy before?"

Matteo looked at his sister with consternation on his face. "And I hope like hell that you haven't either."

She just rolled her eyes. "Matteo, get real. I'm a grown woman."

"With whom? And when? And where?" he said, frowning. "Never mind, I don't want to know."

She shook her head. "Good, cause a girl doesn't kiss and tell."

"What you're talking about goes well beyond kissing."

"Still not gonna talk," she said. "Besides, this isn't about me. Pity the thing. On the one hand, she seems very worldly—she's traveled everywhere. But on the other hand, I mean, hello. That's like Boyfriend 101 material, and she's not gone that far? So that means she hasn't had boyfriends. Which means she must be sexually stunted."

Matteo pinched the bridge of his nose. The last thing he needed right now was to discuss the nonexistent sex life of the woman whose naked body he hadn't been able to forget since the bathtub incident. And now that he knew she'd never shared a bath with another man, well, he was, after all, a goal setter. But no, he shouldn't even think that way, should he?

"How the hell do you even know any of this? I mean, seriously, sexually stunted?" He shook his head in dismay. "Whatever happened to the good old days, when women were seen and not heard?" He slapped her on the back because he knew she'd get totally furious with him for that comment.

"She was commenting on being bathed by someone else for the first time. Shame it was by our old governess." She giggled. "We should have sent in the cabana boy who comes to clean the pool. He'd have worked some magic on her."

"Valentina, the woman had a high fever. She was in no state to engage in any—"

"I'm just playing with you because I can tell it's making

you absolutely crazy, Matteo. I've known you long enough to tell you've got a thing for her whether you'd like to admit it or not. And you're probably thinking Sandro will kill you if you hook up with her, but really, since when did Alessandro dictate your sex life? A certain barmaid from the village comes to mind."

"Oooh, that was a low blow," he said. "You promised you'd never bring her up again after that all got resolved. No more talking about her."

"I'm just saying, you told Sandro where to get off back then, and you'll do it again this time."

"There won't be a this time, this time."

"For your sake, I hope you're wrong, *mio fratello*," she said. "My sweet, naïve brother. Because I know you are just bursting to make your move on this one, and I think you two would be really cute together. What with your little traveling bug and all. When she's all better, you should definitely go for it. And if it pisses Sandro off, then you'll get a two-for-one out of the situation. Now I'm off to find that smelly backpack of hers to see what wonders Allegra can work on it. When she's done, you present that as your mea culpa for anything stupid you might have already said or done to her and voila"—she snapped her fingers—"she'll be eating out of the palm of your hand. And you'll owe me one. Mark my words."

Chapter Fifteen

WORD from above was that Sandro was holding off on beginning the harvest for a few more days. In other words, Matteo had a stay of execution regarding his stowaway.

He'd stopped by Lizzie's room with a surprise.

"Is the coast clear?" he said as he knocked.

He heard a faint assent, so he opened the door. "I've got something that might pass the time a little better."

She turned as he wheeled in a television set.

Her eyes grew wide. "You brought this just for me?"

He nodded. "Not only that, but you'll have satellite, so you're not stuck just watching Italian game shows with naked women."

"I would have thought you'd prefer those."

"Oh, I do," he said, smiling. "But this isn't for me, now, is it?"

She shook her head. "Men."

He took a few minutes to set up the television. "Be careful"—he handed her the remote—"I hear this is a gateway drug."

"It's been so long since I've vegged out in front of a television, I'm not sure I'll know what to do."

"I'm pretty sure it's like riding a horse."

"Another thing I've never done, sadly."

"Wow, you are stunted, aren't you?"

"What does that mean?"

Matteo mentally smacked himself. Of course he was

thinking about the sexually stunted comment from his sister. Damn.

"Nothing," he said. "I was just joking."

She aimed the remote at the television and turned it on, then began scrolling through the hundreds of channels available from all over the world, her eyes wide.

"Wow, I might never leave," she said, settling back into the fluff of pillows but quickly correcting herself. "I mean I'll be out of your hair as soon as I'm up to it."

"Please, stay as long as you wish," he said. "I'd like that. Really."

She lifted her brow. "But didn't you mention something about keeping me away from your ferocious brother? Like he thinks I'm the wine spy or something?"

"It's complicated." He shook his head. "But for now Sandro is focused one hundred percent on determining the precise moment to begin picking. The veraison is continuing quickly. And he will decide with our wine manager exactly when the grapes are perfectly ripe to produce wines with good balance. There needs to be good alcohol content, good acidity, good sugar count, firmness of the grapes, and just the right color. There's much for them to debate and keep him distracted from your presence."

"You lost me at 'veraison,'" she said.

"Ahh, sorry. I figured since you were a wine spy you knew the terminology. Veraison is the color developing in the grape."

"I know exactly nothing about wine," she said with a frown. "I'd sort of hoped to learn a bit about it, though. It's why I came to Chianti when I did."

Matteo feigned indifference in the hopes that she'd

keep talking. "So what's stopping you?"

She shook her head. "Let's just say my plans were interrupted. I guess I'll be forever stuck as a consumer of cheap boxed wines." She sighed.

"That would be tragic," he said. "Once you're better we'll have to fix that. It takes very little to learn anything you'll ever need to know about a good wine."

"Probably not such a great idea as I'll never be able to afford it anyhow."

"Don't you love to learn? Isn't this why you do what you do?"

"What is it that I do?"

"Besides sneaking onto people's property in the middle of the night? I couldn't begin to tell you."

She shrugged. "You got me there."

"My sister mentioned that you've done a lot of traveling. I just assumed someone who traveled a lot would be interested in learning, that's all."

"I'm always on a quest to learn about things, about the world, about people."

"Yet you keep yourself so closed up inside, no one can learn a thing about you."

"Occupational hazard."

"I guess that would be for a wine spy."

She swatted at him. "Stop."

"You know I've done a bit of traveling too."

She raised her eyebrow. "Oh, really?"

He pulled up a chair and sat down next to the bed. If he was going to talk, he'd rather be comfortable. "Yup. I needed to get away and I did. I spent the past year following my instincts, going wherever my heart and head led me."

"So you were chasing a woman?"

He shook his head vigorously. "God, no. I was getting away from one really. By following my heart, I just meant I chose where I yearned to be and went from there."

"Good for you," she said. "Ritz or Four Seasons?"

"Huh?"

"Pretty sure, judging by the spread I've seen so far, you weren't staying at down-and-dirty hostels or surfing on a stranger's couch."

He frowned. "Guilty as charged. Nope. I did not travel in the cheapest of ways. I'm fortunate to be able to stay at amazing hotels and I admit I took advantage of it."

She smiled. "I'm mildly jealous. Though I'd imagine I've had far more memorable 'experiences' than you have thanks to my discount excursions. Traveling broke leads to compromises both good and bad."

"I'd hate to know about some of those experiences," he said. "But I do hope you won't judge me by my means."

"Honestly I'm just impressed that you did that. If I'm guessing correctly, this was stepping way outside your comfort zone. I mean, it would be hard to leave this place ever, am I right?"

"Let's just say that sometimes you have to go far, far away."

She nodded. "You can say that again."

"So now that we're both being cagey about our travel backgrounds, I guess we should switch to a more neutral subject matter, like wine."

"Fair enough. Talk to me about wine."

"Let's start with terroir."

"Whatever that means."

"It's all about this land, the climate, the soil, the

terrain, the tradition. How it affects the taste of the wine you ultimately will enjoy," he said. "This land is magical—it's the land of my blood. My ancestors were doing this very thing hundreds and hundreds of years ago, awaiting the precise moment to pick the grapes for the best wine. Tradition has ensured that our wine is the finest Chianti you'll have."

"So what is your brother so worried about me finding out here?"

He shook his head, frustrated. "Honestly, the grape harvest is hard work: long days stooped over vines, hovered over a bucket, clipping off clusters from stubborn stalks till your hands practically bleed. Your neck hurts, mosquitoes feast on your flesh, gnats blind you as they swarm your head. And the wasps. You're competing with them for their beloved grapes, and they don't give in easily." He smirked.

"On top of all that, you have to listen for the rustle of leaves at your feet that indicates a viper lurking nearby. Usually they're as scared as you, but still, it's a precaution you must be aware of. Your arms begin to ache. Your fingers are stained, your body is dead tired, and you have to get up the next day and do it all again. It's not a relaxing endeavor, to say the least. But growers are very protective of their vines and their grapes—we are professional winemakers, and not just anyone can go out there and do this. The grapes need to be handled tenderly, like a lover. We want no one here who doesn't have the same level of pride in the final product. And I think that's where Alessandro gets very covetous."

"Wow, I didn't realize the politics of grape picking," she said. "The hard work, I get. I've done plenty of equally intense harvesting over the past few years. This sounds far better than some of the chores I've undertaken along the way. Not to mention a piddling little Italian viper couldn't hold a candle to some of the snakes I've encountered. I once saw a cobra when I was working in a rice field in Indonesia. You don't mess with a cobra."

"Better you than me with the snakes," he said, gesturing a definite "no" with his hands. "Not a fan."

"They're great at keeping rodents at bay."

"I prefer feral cats, thanks. But your point is well-taken."

"So talk to me about this winemaking."

"There is much romance that goes into a bottle of wine," he said, his eyes crinkling. "But the true art of winemaking is in the vineyard. If it's not good there, no winemaker can fix it. In the field, a lifetime of experience and knowledge goes into creating the ultimate grape that will make the perfect bottle of wine. And then it comes time to harvest. Determining the ideal moment for picking is an art in itself. As I said, the work of the vendemmia is very hard and sticky, but the end results, perfection."

"Sounds like you've got a great passion for this."

"If you only knew, Lizard. If you only knew."

"So then why did you leave?"

"That, my dear"—he tapped her nose with his finger—"is a story for another day. I think now it's time for your medicine and a nap. I'm sure whatever you find on those five hundred channels will bore you right to sleep. Meantime, if you need me, you can call me on this." He tossed her a two-way radio used all over the farm to communicate from distances. "And I'll come running."

Sometimes he hated himself for being such a sucker

for a hard-to-get woman.

Chapter Sixteen

LIZZIE settled under the blankets and gorged for a while on cable news until she remembered why she hated cable news and turned off the television and closed her eyes. She'd been holed up in a room with the shutters closed, and Italian shutters were most effective at keeping any hint of daylight at bay. So barring looking at a clock, she'd never know if it was ten in the morning or the middle of the night.

She drifted off to sleep, feeling oddly settled for the first time in ages. It was a strange sensation for her, but it felt almost right. She closed her eyes as she thought about her conversation with Matteo and how surprisingly lovely it had been, and soon she melted into a deep sleep.

It would have been nice for those thoughts to grab hold in her dreams, but instead, she was revisited by that sensation of fear and lack of control that she didn't realize had her in its icy grip. When her guard was down, that fright insinuated itself into her dreams, with a drunk and monstrous Luigi racing after her, tripping her, pinning her facedown in the mud where she thrashed and cried out for help but knew there was no one around to save her from whatever he wanted to do to her. In her dreams, she was in the very bed in which she was sleeping, but Luigi had found her and was forcing his way beneath the blankets.

She woke with a start in the dark, her breathing clipped, her mind racing as she tried to remember where she was and if she was safe. She recalled her conversation with Matteo and fumbled around the nightstand for the two-way radio. She felt weak but her need for a sense of safety and reassurance eclipsed her usual insistence on complete autonomy.

"Matteo," she said, panic in her voice. "I need you. Please, come, now."

Matteo had been assessing the veraison in one of the vineyards when he received a panicked call from Lizzie.

"I'll be right there," he said, taking off at a run.

He didn't bother to knock when he made it to her room, instead bursting in and flicking on the overhead lights.

"Are you okay? What's happened?"

Lizzie was sitting up in bed, trembling. "He was there... I mean here... in my dreams. He was right here and I couldn't scream. I couldn't move. There was nothing I could do to stop him."

"Who is he?" he said, nudging her with his hip so that she would make room for him on the mattress. He sat and wrapped his arms around her to soothe her. "It's okay now, Lizzie. You're safe here." He stroked her hair with his hand to gentle her.

Her breathing settled down and she let out a deep sigh. "I didn't realize how afraid I still was," she said, quietly sobbing. "I'm so afraid."

"Is this Hamilton? Are you ready to tell me about

him?"

She leaned out of his arms and stared at him with a strange look of confusion on her face. "Huh?"

"I know something bad happened to you," he said. "And I think it has to do with some man named Hamilton. You talked about things in your sleep that first day when you were so sick with fever."

She knit her brow, pressing her memory, trying to put together what he was talking about. "Hamilton?"

"I don't really know what was going on up here," he said, tapping her head. "But you kept talking in your sleep. At one point you shouted out for someone to stop. You even screamed, 'Leave me alone, you bastard. Get out of my bed!' and flailed your arms as if you were fighting someone. And then you said 'I surrender.' I think your exact words were: 'I surrender. I'm yours.' As if that wasn't strange enough, you kept muttering about Hamilton. And some woman named Lynn."

Lizzie blanched and she seemed to freeze momentarily. Once she collected herself, she heaved another big sigh and sat up straighter in bed, wiping away the tears that had pooled in her eyes.

"Be prepared to be bored."

"Try me."

"You'll be asleep in a matter of minutes."

"I could use a good nap."

"So I came to Tuscany to join in the vendemmia. It sounded exciting, and I thought it would be a great education, learning about winemaking. I knew it was hard to do that with no experience. But I had heard you could sign on with small farms, where they might not follow the official regulations like at the big vineyards. As a newbie, I knew I couldn't get real work anywhere harvesting grapes. But Fattoria Luigi sounded great on paper. It was a small vineyard, run by this selfsame Luigi. From our e-mail exchanges, everything sounded charming and quintessentially Italian.

"It wasn't till I arrived there that I learned he wasn't true to his word. He'd said there would be transportation for me to come and go, but that turned out to be a rusted bike with two flat tires. The 'fresh Italian meals' he promised ended up being rotting vegetables and tins of tuna fish. None of those satisfying five-course meals with wine after a hard day of harvesting."

Fuming, Matteo was about ready to burst a blood vessel in his head. "Who is this Luigi person? I want to find him and straighten him out. What kind of man would offer such hospitality?"

"Oh, trust me, it gets worse," she said. "So I was the only worker, though he made it sound like the place would be filled with young people like me. Instead of harvesting grapes, he had me doing hard labor all day long. And finally after a few days of this, I went to bed, absolutely dead tired. Unfortunately the sleeping quarters were in keeping with the rest of his lies: his 'guest shed' made your toolshed look like a five-star hotel. Being used to low-end accommodations, I dealt with it. But what I wasn't used to was when Luigi—who spent his days getting drunk—decided to visit me, uninvited, in the middle of the night. I was sound asleep, but thank God I reacted quickly and elbowed him so hard in the gut, he was stunned. I jumped out of bed, grabbed my things, and ran out of the house."

Matteo frowned, quiet for a minute, nodding as it all started to make sense. "And after you wandered around the roads in the dark, it started to rain, and you ended up finding a toolshed to sleep in. And then a complete asshole guy startled you awake before dawn and gave you a fat heap of shit when all you were doing was trying to protect yourself," he said, a tear finding its way from his eye. "Lizzie, I'm so sorry. I'm so very sorry. Why didn't you tell me? Why did you let me be such a prick to you? And then you were so sick, and I was such a heartless bastard."

Lizzie held up her hands. "No, really, Matteo, it's not a big deal." She swallowed and continued, her voice stronger this time. "I told you, I'm really independent and I am always on the go. It didn't matter. I was planning to be out of there before anyone showed up. I'd just hoped to sleep a little longer, maybe let my clothes dry a bit more."

"But you didn't deserve to be treated like a criminal. Which is what I did. Instead of being empathetic and asking you what was wrong and how you found yourself there, I just attacked you."

"I'd say you made up for it," she said, spreading her arms out to indicate the luxurious bedroom she'd taken over as her own.

"I'm such a dick," he said.

"No, really. Luigi, he's a dick. You were just protecting your grapes."

"You do know that sounds especially stupid under the circumstances."

"You were being a good Romeo."

"Which is not always an easy thing to do."

"Seems like the sort of place where it's easy to be perfect."

He shook his head. "Looks are sometimes deceiving. Things are not always as they appear from the outside. Yes, we're a loving family. And yes, we have many blessings to be thankful for. But we have had our tragedy, and we all dealt with it in ways that didn't always fit together so well."

He looked down at his lap, his shoulders slumped. "You see, my father died unexpectedly when I was a teenager. It shocked us all, and instead of pulling together we despaired. And in that deep, deep sadness, we couldn't find it in us to be there for each other but rather fought at every turn. Alessandro, as the oldest, took it upon himself to replace Papà, but I for one resented that he dared think he could replace our father. Sandro acted as if he was in charge of our every breathing moment, which I rejected flat out. And while he took over the day-to-day operations of the winery, he controlled things more and more tightly, so much so that the rest of us felt like useless appendages. Things came to a head last year when Sandro failed to support me after I was wrongly accused of some things. I couldn't take it anymore, so I left. I needed to get away and figure out if I had it in me to be part of Romeo wines, or if I wanted to do something completely new and Romeo-free with my life."

"And did you decide?"

"Let's say the decision is a work in progress," he said. "Which means I have no idea. Because the reality is that my brother, as the firstborn, is as royal as you'll get in modern Italy. He replaced my father as the marchese, which I think is what you would call a 'marquis.' So the Cantine dei Marchese Romeo, makers of some of the best Chiantis Italy has to offer? It's really Sandro's as he's the figurehead for the label. The rest of us? We're left to be his grunts. Or at least that's what he makes it feel like."

"I'm sorry, Matteo," she said. "To have all of this but

to not have it must be very bittersweet."

"It'll work out," he said. "But I want to talk more about you. Like why are you always running? And who is Hamilton? And that woman Lynn?"

Lizzie burst out laughing. "Honestly you really don't want to know about Hamilton. Or Lin, for that matter."

"But I do," he said. "You were so troubled. It worried me. But, yet in the middle of your bad dreams, you told him you surrendered, which made no sense."

"Trust me, Hamilton is entirely uninteresting. Not worth bringing up."

"Please, Lizzie," he said. "I've been wondering what affected you so deeply that you cried out in your sleep."

He didn't dare mention what she'd said about Italian men. Or this Hamilton's chest. At last he had this bird chirping and he didn't want to prevent her from making a clean breast of things. And he wouldn't dare suggest the way he'd like to clean those breasts, which might just involve that fantasy bath he couldn't stop thinking about, much to his chagrin.

Chapter Seventeen

"**HAVE** you heard about that Broadway play, *Hamilton?*" Lizzie said, looking down and avoiding eye contact.

Matteo shook his head. "Doesn't ring any bells for me."

She exhaled and glanced up. "So... there's this actor, and well, he's also a writer, and, honestly, he's a lot of things," she said. "And he has this hugely successful play on Broadway and he's been in the news a lot and I guess somewhere along the line I saw him on YouTube. And, well, he's very interesting."

"So his name is Hamilton?"

She shook her head. "No, his name is Lin. Lin-Manuel Miranda."

"Ahhh, so this Lynn is a man?"

"Yes, exactly," she said. "I suppose when I saw you, something about you reminded me of him, so maybe when I was hallucinating with that high fever, I conflated the two of you or something. I don't really know. But it's no big deal."

He paused for a second, steepling his fingers as he thought about this. "So you mistook me for this actor, then?"

Lizzie creased her brow. "Not necessarily. Why do you ask?"

"I just wondered because of some other things you'd said."

Her cheeks reddened and she glanced to either side as though were seeking an escape hatch. "What might that have been? I mean people say crazy things when they're sick. Something about the high temperatures, I think I read one time. It messes with your brain, you know?"

He grinned. "I bet it does." He loved it when the pieces of a puzzle started to fall into place. The best part was fitting the easy pieces together, and when you worked on the ones that were so elusive and thought it impossible to know where they belonged, everything suddenly fit. "I seem to recall you saying something about always loving Italian men. And then about that hair, that smile, that chest. And then something to do with your hands gladly wandering over that chest."

Lizzie's stared at him wide-eyed. "I did not say that!"

"I'm afraid so." He nodded with fake reluctance. "But of course, like you said, a high fever makes your brain do crazy things, I'm sure."

Lizzie slid down beneath the comforter. "I could about die," she said with a groan.

Matteo lifted the blanket so he could see her face, but she pulled it back, covering her face again. "There's no need to feel bad about that. You can't help what you say when you're asleep. Especially when you were so sick."

She lifted a part of the blanket so that one eye was visible. "You think so?"

Matteo smiled. "I tell you what," he said. "It'll be our secret. No one will ever be the wiser. We can pretend it never happened."

She moaned, rolling over onto her side, her back toward him. "But it did," she said. "And it's obvious I was talking about you. But I didn't even know I was. And now you know."

"You were talking about me?" he said, hoping to lure her out from her blanket cave.

She pulled the blanket down and turned to look at him. "You didn't think that's what I was doing? And then I go and say it out loud, so now you do? Now I could really die."

Matteo slipped beneath the blanket and wrapped his arms around her, pulling her close.

"Please don't die, Lizard," he said. "I just spent all this time trying to keep you alive. It wouldn't be right if you died now."

"Really?" she said, not looking at him. "You don't want to laugh at me for being such an idiot?"

"As a matter of fact, I'd much rather do this," he said, nuzzling her neck, his fingers gently scratching her scalp. "But I don't want to be presumptuous, Lizzie. It's just that ever since I saw you in such a pathetic state standing there in our toolshed, I've had the strangest desire to kiss you."

She rolled over to face him. "You know I'm sick, don't you? You don't want to get my sick germs."

"The doctor told me you most likely aren't contagious," he said. "Besides, you've been on an antibiotic long enough for me not to have to worry. In any event, I'll take my chances."

Matteo pulled her to him, his hand gently pressing her head toward his as he bent down and placed a soft kiss on her lips. She responded by deepening the kiss, opening her lips to him, and he slid his tongue along the edge of her lips, searching for her tongue, his hands roaming across her back as he pressed his body to hers.

He closed his eyes and breathed in the amazing

sensation of having this woman in his arms, his mouth on hers, knowing he was exactly where he was supposed to be at this moment in time. Although she was indeed sick, and probably the last thing she should be doing right now was overheating herself making out with him, he couldn't help himself. Everything just felt so right. *She* felt so right. His hands grazed her warm skin beneath the silky top of her borrowed pajamas, sending a chill of sensual pleasure through him. He slid a hand across her breast, tweaking her already hard nipple, and she groaned her approval.

"More," she said.

"We've got to take it slowly," he said. "Your body can't take too much exertion right now."

"But I'm pretty sure this is just what the doctor ordered to make me feel better."

"Does it feel good?"

She moaned. "You can't imagine how good."

He nipped at her chin, at her neck, at that sensitive part at the base of her throat, and then he pulled down the neckline of her pajamas to expose a tight, rosy nipple. He dragged his tongue across the tip before settling his mouth over hers, sucking and gently biting as she pressed her hips toward his, his erection unmistakably present between them. She reached down and stroked it atop his jeans. God, he wanted nothing between them but skin on skin.

Matteo was so lost in worshipping Lizzie's body that he forgot about what happens when you're caught up in that first mind-blowing embrace, followed by one incredible kiss, topped off by whispered promises. You get lost in it. So lost that you might not notice what's going on around you.

But then, in what seemed like some other universe, he

suddenly heard the distinctive sound of a throat clearing. That was impossible. He and Lizzie were the only ones in the room. But he heard it again, and he reluctantly lifted his head away from her to see none other than his brother Sandro standing at the foot of the bed, arms crossed, fingers drumming a judgmental beat on his arms.

Fuck.

"So this is how we treat our sick houseguests?" he said, not even disguising the disgust in his voice. "I'd expect nothing more from you, Matteo. Get your ass out of that bed. Now."

Chapter Eighteen

SPEAKING of dying of embarrassment, if this didn't kill Lizzie, nothing would. How could she have gone from Bedridden Betty to Horny Hannah in the blink of an eye? And then to have the infamous Sandro break them up just as Matteo had his mouth firmly planted on her left breast (which felt so insanely amazing, damn that brother of his for being such a buzzkill). She'd never live this down.

Though since she would be out of here in oh, an hour, it would be her own mortifying secret, and she'd eventually get past it. There'd be no one around to hold that against her. She wouldn't have to see any of these Romeos ever again. Thank goodness.

Except she wasn't being truthful with herself because there was one damn Romeo who had somehow gotten under—and on top of—her fevered skin. And she was instantly sad at the idea of never seeing him again, not to mention never doing some more of *that* with the man.

Let's face it, *that* had been like nothing she'd ever experienced before, and she suspected this was just a small sampling of what he had to offer her. She'd only had the appetizer and she wanted the all-you-can-eat buffet, which was clearly what she hungered for, even though she hadn't realized it. She'd been starving for so long, she'd forgotten what it was like to crave a man like that. Or maybe she'd never really known.

Meanwhile, Matteo had stood in a flash the minute

Sandro opened his mouth, and Lizzie could see the bulge in his jeans, unmistakable evidence of their prior actions. It triggered a yearning in the pit of her stomach so powerful she almost wanted to cry. Then again, perhaps it was because of her horror at what his brother witnessed.

She didn't even know how to react and lay there mortified as Matteo started yelling at his brother, making it abundantly clear what he thought of his actions.

"*Vaffanculo*," he said, his face red with rage. "Fuck you, Sandro. Who the hell do you think you are coming in here like that?"

"I should ask you that question, 'coming' in here like that," Sandro said. "Who do you think you are, assaulting a vulnerable houseguest?"

"Assaulting?" Matteo said, his voice jumping several octaves. "Are you fucking kidding me?"

Lizzie raised her hand. "Uh, he wasn't assaulting me."

They both turned to look at her, Matteo giving her a tight smile and a reassuring wink.

"You," Sandro said, pointing at her. "Be quiet."

Lizzie gasped and glared at him.

Matteo grabbed his brother by the shoulder. "Don't you dare talk to her like that."

"Don't you tell me what to say," Sandro said, his nostrils flaring. "You go hiding some, some *intruder* in our home, thinking I won't notice it, and you have the nerve to tell me what not to say to her?"

"I'm this close to losing it altogether." Matteo held his fingers an inch apart. "Get out of here now, Sandro. You will not discuss this in front of my friend and insult her like this. Get out now." He shoved his brother hard, following him out the door.

Lizzie had never felt so horrible in her whole life. Well, except the day she found out her father had been killed. And she'd never had a chance to say good-bye to him. That ranked up there as the worst day ever. And when she learned her mother was marrying his best friend, yeah, that hurt a lot.

But this? Now? This was flat-out, down-and-dirty humiliation. And the crazy thing is she had no idea how this all transpired so quickly. She went from being attacked by that horrid man, to being desperately sick, to going to second base (Is that where they were? She was not up on her baseball–make-out session terminology) with Matteo, who she'd probably have happily slapped across the face a day ago for being so rude. Now, though, she missed having his mouth on her in a truly bad way.

She heard them yelling outside the door and wanted to go out there and defend Matteo. What he did was nothing but gentlemanly. Well, what he just did was nothing but manly. In only the best of ways. But taking her in and caring for her? It showed her that he was a good man, and his brother needed to cut him some slack.

She held her ear to the door to listen. She thought about getting a glass from the bathroom so she could hear better. Maybe she was a spy after all. Didn't they use drinking glasses to eavesdrop?

"I'm sick and tired of you thinking that just because you were the oldest when Papà died, that you own us all," he said. "He didn't die and make you boss—*you* made yourself boss, and I for one am sick of it." No doubt that was Matteo shouting.

"You're lucky I did that or you wouldn't be standing in this house right now, enjoying the lifestyle afforded you because I I filled his shoes."

"Pardon me for not being old enough to do that then," Matteo said. "But I am now. Every last one of us is old enough now to contribute our share in the care and running of this vineyard, but you won't let go of a damn thing. Do you know how that makes us feel?"

"How do you think I feel, Matteo," his brother said, "when you all got to go off and have a childhood? You just continued your lives as if nothing even happened. And you had the chance to go on to university as well. And travel the continent. And wine and dine with friends, and have an all-around good time while I was holding it all together."

"No one asked you to that, mio fratello," Matteo said. "You did that for whatever reason drove you to do so. How can you blame us when you never put it to us all to decide? You took on the burden and now you blame us for the rest of our lives? How reasonable is that?"

"You know Mamma couldn't handle things," Sandro responded, his voice tight. "All those children, this huge business, and having just lost the love of her life. Mamma needed me. And no, I wasn't going to ask anyone permission. I did what I needed to do."

"Fine, Sandro. And we're all grateful for it. But it wasn't a license to blame us for the rest of our lives, nor did this grant you permission to keep us at arm's length while you ran the vineyard. You've heard the saying that many hands make light work? Yet you reject the lightening of the load, so certain we're incapable of doing it right. As if we can't honor Papà's legacy as well as you."

"When you do things like you did, bringing in that woman just as we're about to harvest the grapes, that shows me you're not thinking like a Romeo," he said.

"That woman was someone who was in deep need. Of course I was going to help her out. I'm not a heartless jerk. Besides, I can assure you our father would have done the same thing. He didn't covet his wine to the exclusion of helping out someone who needed some TLC."

Lizzie had had enough. She was perfectly capable of standing up for herself and not letting Matteo have to carry the water for her. She opened the door and stood with her legs spread, hands on her waist. She'd read if you stood like Superman, it would afford you superpowers, and she felt like she needed all the support she could muster. Besides, she wasn't feeling all that fantastic. This stress was bringing her down, and she needed to keep her reserves so that she could get the hell out of here.

"Look, Sandro," she said. "I'm afraid we haven't had the pleasure of formally meeting. And it looks as if we never will. Oh, well, your loss. I apologize if my presence has posed some sort of existential threat to your family's well-being. Quite frankly my life has never seemed so important as it does now that an entire family must want to bring me down to save their empire. I guess I can consider I've made it now that I'm part of some evil cabal I never knew existed. But you know what? Maybe you could stop taking yourself so damned seriously and recognize that you have a family that loves you, a brother who has a lot to contribute to Romeo wines or whatever you call yourselves, and you're squandering this amazing resource because you're too busy nursing that stick that is wedged so far up your ass. Thanks for your attention. I'll be packing and leaving as soon as I can find my belongings. It's been real. Peace out."

Lizzie hadn't noticed that all the shouting had drawn

an audience, and no sooner than she finished her soliloquy, she realized a stunning older woman, with dark hair generously sprinkled with gray strands, stood off to the side. She had a smile spread across her kind face and wore an apron covered with food stains over her dress and scuffy worn-down slippers. Next to her stood Valentina, her arm raised, spinning her fist in a circular "you go, girl" motion. The two of them stood and applauded, Valentina adding a few catcall whistles for good measure.

Lizzie turned beet red. Not simply because she'd just read Matteo's brother the riot act, but because she was standing in the—very elegant, tastefully appointed—hallway in her bare feet and skimpy pajamas. She crossed her arms across her chest, a nod to about as much modesty as she could drum up under the circumstances.

"Oh, honey, that was absolutely amazing," Valentina said. "Wasn't it, Mamma?"

Her mother nodded. "So this is Lizzie the Lizard?" she said to her daughter. "So lovely to meet you, dear. I'm Fabiana." She embraced Lizzie in a warm hug. "I've heard so much about you."

"Thank you so much," Lizzie said. "I'm really sorry about insulting your son. I'm just going to collect my things and get out of your way."

"You'll do no such thing," Fabiana said. "You are our guest in this house for as long as you'd like to stay. You can even help with the vendemmia if you'd like. I'd be happy to have your assistance."

Sandro's eyes about bugged out of his head.

"Mamma—"

She held her hand up to silence him. "Don't Mamma me." Her tone was sharp. "You've been terribly rude to

Matteo's friend and you need to apologize to her. This is not how a Romeo acts and you should know better."

Poor Lizzie couldn't erase the memory of looking up to see Matteo's brother staring at them and being caught red-handed. Or red-mouthed.

Sandro grimaced and glanced at the floor. "I suppose I have to apologize to you."

"Sandro Romeo, that is not an apology," his mother said.

He toed his shoe into the Oriental rug that was probably from the Renaissance. "Okay. Fine. I'm sorry."

"Now shake hands and introduce yourself to her as you would any houseguest," his mother said.

He rolled his eyes but reached out his hand nonetheless. "I'm Sandro Romeo," he said quietly.

"And I'm Taylor McFarland," came a voice turning a nearby corner. Lizzie looked up—and up and up—to see a towering beauty of a woman, blond and suntanned and about as wholesome and all-American as they came. "Has Sandro been behaving badly?"

Several heads nodded in unison and Taylor shook hers. "Please, accept my apologies on Sandro's behalf." She shook Lizzie's hand. "I take it you're the 'wine spy'?" she said, making air quotes to show she was teasing him for his paranoid presumptions about Lizzie.

"Alas, not even a wine snob." Lizzie smiled. "Just plain old Lizzie Moretti. But great to meet you."

"Really, Sandro has a heart of gold," Taylor said. "Just sometimes, it seems like it's encased in a thin layer of lead."

"I'm so glad you two got to meet," Valentina said. "Because Taylor and I have designs on you, Lizzie."

Lizzie frowned, not knowing what the hell that meant.

"Oh, nothing bad," she said. "We just thought we'd take you out to get a little girlie-girled up. Thought it would be a nice treat after everything you've been through."

They'd been talking about her? Was that good or was that weird? Perhaps that wasn't a weird thing, considering she was something new and different in the Romeo household. New blood. Or new meat, depending on how she chose to look at it. But Valentina seemed to be delightful, and the mere fact that Taylor came right up and dope-slapped Sandro, well, that made her okay too. Maybe making a few girlfriends at this point wouldn't be such a bad thing, after all.

Chapter Nineteen

MATTEO'S mother insisted Lizzie join the family for dinner and far be it for her to turn down the invitation. She was tired but wasn't feeling quite as awful as before and could just as easily sit at a dinner table as in a bed.

"But—" she said, pointing down to her clothes or lack thereof.

"I'm on it," Valentina said. "Give me five minutes and I'll scare something up for you to wear."

"You don't have to do that," Lizzie said. "Really, I can just wear something from my pack, if I could just find it."

Valentina cocked a brow. "Uh, about that." She glanced at her mother as they both suppressed a giggle. "Allegra's been trying to clean everything, but so far, it all smells pretty awful. She's soaking your clothes in vinegar, but you might want to keep your distance until she's able to do something to mitigate the stench. Have faith, though. She's perfected veritable miracles with laundry."

Lizzie pouted. Not that she was terribly attached to her things, but it was all she had.

"Like I said, Taylor and I plan to have our wicked way with you as soon as you're up to a day out. We'll get you all fixed up."

Shame, the idea of another Romeo having his wicked way with her sounded more immediately appealing.

Matteo looped his arm through Lizzie's. "In the meantime, if you'll do me the honors of allowing me to escort you back to your quarters." She smiled up at him. Hope sprung eternal.

"We'll see you all at dinnertime."

The group dissipated as the two of them walked back into the bedroom. Lizzie closed the door behind her and leaned against it, her arms and legs spread as if keeping a mob from storming the place. "Well, that was one way to meet the family," she said.

Matteo reached for her hand and grabbed it between both of his. "That was really quite amazing," he said. "Never have I seen someone shut down Alessandro Romeo like that. You did an amazing job standing your ground. I was so proud of how you handled that."

Lizzie winced, the realization of what she'd said hitting her. "I didn't know what I was doing," she said. "I was just so annoyed at how he was treating you. It was wrong of him to box you into a corner like that and to treat you so disrespectfully. I can see how you're frustrated with him."

"It's complicated," he said. "He has valid points about his role in saving the family business. He is, after all, the self-appointed principal of the world-famous Cantine dei Marchesi Romeo winemakers. Our family has a history of winemaking that extends back over six hundred years, back in the days of Italian nobility. The Romeos were as royal as they came in Italy. Even now we have direct ties to the royal family in Monaforte—our Mamma's brother is married to the queen. I suppose Sandro feels a deep responsibility to our ancestors to get it right."

"The closest I've gotten to royalty is the vintage Royal typewriter I inherited from my father. But then I lost the thing when my mother moved in with his best friend and purged anything she thought we didn't need."

"Wow. That's harsh. Why did she do that?"

Lizzie sighed. "I wish I could tell you. When my father died, she totally shut down. She was a military wife and spent many years following orders like she was expected to do. But she expected he'd return home, and when he didn't, she didn't handle it well. It's hard for me to criticize her, but it was hard for all of us. And then she ended up getting together with my father's best friend and they were married practically before the grass had grown over my father's grave."

"That must have been hard for you." He pulled her in for a hug.

She nodded. "Pretty life defining, actually. It was then I decided to take off. Made no sense to stick around at that point. And by then my brother had decided to 'honor' my father by joining the army. Considering how that worked out for my dad, well, let's just say I was less than enthusiastic. I realized it was hard work caring about people, so I decided to take a bit of a hiatus from that."

"And so you took your show on the road."

"Yup."

There was a knock on the door and the two separated, not wanting any more prying eyes on them.

"A change of clothes for you," Valentina said in a singsongy voice. She placed the clothes she was carrying on the bed. "A comfy sweater, a pair of black slacks—stretchy, so you'll have room for dessert—and black flats. I figured no need to accessorize—it is, after all, just dinner with us. We'll take care of that when you're ready for the two of us."

Matteo laughed. "Shopping with those two will be like a hunting expedition in the savanna. You'll need to be prepared for arduous work and it will require all of your concentration."

Valentina smacked him playfully on the shoulder. "You just can't appreciate the fine art of acquiring." She winked at Lizzie. "And now, I'll leave you to it. Whatever *it* is. *A presto.*" She elbowed her brother in the ribs, and he rolled his eyes at the subtlety of the maneuver, closing and locking the door behind her.

"So, you've had a bit of family for a day, I suppose. And you've still got four more to meet."

"Four more? Good Lord, your parents were busy. Seven of you total?"

"Yep. Francesco, Domenico, Lorenzo, and Tomasso are somewhere around here. Hard to know who will be here for dinner, but you'll definitely have a chance to meet them before—"

"Before I leave," she said. "Which will be as soon as I get my things back. I've more than overstayed my welcome here."

"You haven't even begun to do that. You saw my mother and my sister. And Taylor. You're the belle of the ball. Clearly we needed some new blood in the place, and you're it."

"I'm honored, really I am. But this is your family, and I don't want to insert myself in the middle of things."

"Shhhh," Matteo said, holding his finger to her lips. "No more protesting. Why don't you get changed and I'll entertain myself with this exciting television?"

"How long until dinner?"

He looked at his watch. "Two hours. Plenty of time."

"I was hoping you'd say that," she said. "Because I could use some help."

He lifted an eyebrow. "Oh?"

"I really need to take a bath, considering I've been feverish in bed and all…"

Chapter Twenty

SURELY Matteo hadn't heard Lizzie correctly. Impossible that she'd just said what he'd desperately hoped for.

"You want me to get Allegra?" he said. "She's probably cooking dinner, but maybe I could see if my sister could take over for her."

He walked over to the bedroom door.

"Wait," Lizzie said. "Please. Don't go. I hear I've been missing out on something. Maybe you can show me what that is."

I love my sister. Matteo barely suppressed a smile.

She held out her hand and he twined his fingers with hers.

It seemed forever for the tub to fill with water. Lizzie seemed twitchy—she'd likely never done anything like this before. He looked at her warmly, hoping to ease her nervousness.

"Here," he said. "Let me help you with this."

He reached for the hem of her camisole top and slid it up over her head. She blushed, standing there nearly naked.

"Let's make it even," she said as she pulled his shirt over his head as well. When she glimpsed his shirtless body, she inhaled sharply and reached out before running her fingers lightly through his chest hair.

"I like even," he said. "But even more, I like removing things that are just in the way. So give me that."

Matteo looped his fingers in the waistband of the small

satin shorts and easily slipped them down her legs till they pooled at her feet. He stood and took his fill of her striking body.

"Are you sure you're up for this?" he said, pointing at her and then at himself. "I mean, you, me, now? I don't want to wear you out."

She smiled. "I have a feeling it would be worth it. But don't worry. I'll tell you if I hit my limit. In the meantime, gimme those things."

She pulled at his belt to loosen it, unbuttoned his jeans, and skimmed them off along with his black boxer trunks.

"I can't believe I'm standing here naked with a man I just met days ago," she said.

"It does seem strange," he said. "But it seems like that was a lifetime ago."

"'Met,' if you can call it that." She laughed. "More like accosted."

"You haven't seen accosted yet, Miss Lizzie Moretti," he said, holding her hand as he helped her lower into the tub. "By the time I'm done with you…"

She blushed. "I'm kind of new at this game if you hadn't noticed."

"It's really quite simple. Even easier than riding a horse. First, you settle in." He nestled behind her in the large tub so that she was comfortably sitting in the crook of his lap. "Then you let the mood take over."

He reached for the soap and lathered his hands, then slipped them around Lizzie, working his slippery hands over her breasts till she moaned from the pleasure of it.

"See?" he said. "Easy peasy."

He soaped up his hands some more and slid them

down her body.

"You must take care to get even the hard-to-reach areas," he said, his fingers sliding between her legs, easily gliding back and forth along her slick center.

Lizzie pressed her bottom against his erection, rolling her hips as Matteo worked his fingers worked inside of her and pressed in a circular motion around her clit.

"Just lay your head against my shoulder and let me do all the work," he said as his other hand played with her breast.

"That... doesn't seem... fair to make you do... everything." She gasped as he continued.

"Trust me, I'm very happy with my job right now."

"And I'm very happy you only had a bathtub in this room."

"Ahhh, but have no fear. I can work even more magic in a shower once you graduate from bathtubs. I'll be sure to show you sometime soon."

Lizzie's breath was coming faster and she ground her bottom rhythmically against his hard cock, pressing herself against his fingers.

"Ohhh, Matteo, that. Right there," she said, panting hard. "Oh, my God, please don't stoppppp." She let out a yelp he worried would bring someone running, but it was short-lived as she thrust herself hard against his fingers, pressing them deeper into her, where he could feel her muscles clenching on him. He held tight to her as her climax hit over and over again seemingly in waves.

Exhausted and sated, she slumped against his body.

He stroked his fingers through her hair and turned her so she was sideways across his lap, and he held her tightly against his chest.

"I could get used to this," he said.

"Don't get too comfortable." She turned to him, eyes twinkling. "You didn't think I'd forget about you, did you?"

She shifted her body so that she straddled him and began to slide her center over his erection, back and forth like her life depended on it. Their mouths met and mimicked what Matteo was desperate to do *there*.

"Do you have anything?" she said.

He quickly did the mental math and remembered he had a condom in his wallet. Thank God.

"Can you reach for my pants? Right there, and if you can hand me my wallet in the pocket."

He quickly extracted the prize and tore the wrapper in record time. "Now, what say you slide this on me and then slide you on me, okay, baby? I need to feel your wet body around me."

Lizzie fumbled with the condom at first but got the thing on, then settled herself, his cock poised at her opening. Ever so slowly she pressed down on top of him as if savoring the moment, till finally—finally—he was seated inside of her warmth.

"God, Lizzie, we fit so perfectly," he said. It probably wasn't fair to make her do all the work now but he was so content feeling the warm glide of their bodies together and watching her breasts bounce as she lifted and lowered herself back on him. He took one of them into his mouth and sucked hard, which prompted her to move faster. Up and down, around and around she pressed herself to him so he was buried as deep as he could be.

"Oh, Matteo, I'm going to come again—keep doing that to me."

"You're doing it all, Lizzie girl," he said. "It's so good,

just a few more strokes and I'm right there with you—" He groaned onto her nipple, his own vibrations being all it took for her to go over the edge again, this time letting out a yell so piercing he had to cover her mouth with his hand.

"I love that you get so excited." He stroked her breasts. "We just don't want anyone to call the ambulance on you."

The water had lost much of its warmth. But neither of them felt like moving, so they curled into each other and lay there, supremely contented.

"My Lizard," he said, twisting her hair between his fingers, his voice trailing off. "Do you think maybe I could call you something a little more affectionate, like 'kitten'? *Gattino*. I like that."

"Oh, I don't know," she said. "Lizard does have a certain cachet to it. I'll leave it up to you."

"All I know is you passed the bath lessons with flying colors. You are most definitely ready to take on the shower next, gattino."

"I'm at your mercy."

If only Matteo could count on that. But somehow he knew that wasn't the case.

Chapter Twenty-One

SANDRO had proclaimed it was time for the harvest to begin, which meant Lizzie was stuck inside while everyone else enjoyed the glorious autumn day picking grapes. Though from what she'd heard, maybe it wasn't the easiest of jobs.

Valentina came in for a bathroom break moaning about her beautiful manicure.

"What was I thinking having my nails done just in time for the vendemmia? You'd think I was a rookie or something."

"Maybe you should wear gloves?" Lizzie said.

"Oh, but I do," she said. "You just can't seem to get away from the purple stains. Hazard of the job."

"Well, then, when this is over, you'd best get back to your manicurist and make them look gorgeous again."

"And you're coming along," she said.

"I don't know, Valentina," she said. "I'm going to need to get a move on soon."

"You keep saying that but no, you don't. You can stay here as long as you want."

"I know you all say that, but really, after awhile old houseguests start to smell like week-old fish."

"You mean like that backpack of yours?"

Lizzie frowned. "That bad?"

Valentina scrunched her nose. "Worse."

"Allegra's had no luck with it?"

"She sent it to her sister in Siena. She's supposedly even better at cleaning laundry than Allegra. So sorry, looks like you're stuck here."

"There could be worse places to be trapped."

On Friday night, the family went into Santa Romeo for the Festa dell'uva, the annual grape harvest festival. All the vineyards, small and large, celebrated with tastings and food, music, and dancing.

As Lizzie and the Romeo clan drew near, the crowds grew thick. And the unmistakable smell of fermenting grapes hung in the air.

"The streets," Lizzie said, "they're stained purple."

Matteo smiled. "Spillage from the pressings. I love it—it's an integral part of the vendemmia. And soon to come, the olive harvest. You picked the best time to be in Chianti."

Tables were set up in the piazza, along with Italian flags and banners for all of the local *cantine*. The town's unofficial mayor was adorned with his *il Tricolore* green, white, and red sash, in the colors of the Italian flag.

People were dancing and singing and happy to share in the fun. As they walked through the piazza, Matteo was greeted by many friends. It made her almost jealous to not truly be a part of the festivities. Even if she'd stayed at Luigi's, she'd have participated in it. Now she was a bystander. Not that she'd have stayed there. But it was her only chance at that brass ring. So instead, she'd have to settle for outsider status.

She'd watched from the terrace each day as the workers and the Romeos picked grapes and filled the buckets and moved them onto trucks that would take them to be crushed for the fermentation process. It was obviously hard work; she could hear people complaining about their backs and the hot sun and the wasps that were able to sting right through the picking gloves. But hardships over farmwork were nothing new to her. It would have just been more enjoyable to be part of it.

Since she was still getting over being sick, Lizzie refrained from consuming much wine—she didn't want to risk making the antibiotic less effective, though the doctor told her Italians had been taking both for many years.

"I'm going to get a bottle of wine," Matteo said. "Can I get you anything?"

"Nope, I'm good," she said, happy to be off her feet for a few minutes. She watched as Valentina took turns dancing with a few of her brothers.

Then she felt a familiar churn in her stomach as a voice rang out by her ear. "Ahhh… *la strega Americano*," Luigi said, his sour, fermented breath on her so close she felt nauseous. The American witch, he called her. The bastard.

"You'd best leave me alone or I will get the polizia involved," she said. But looking at him, she was reminded why she was duly frightened by him: he was a large, powerful man who could easily pin her down and hurt her.

"The poor American girl, couldn't take it? I was too much loving for you?"

Her stomach curdled at the thought. She glanced at the contingent of Romeos dancing, but none were looking her way, the music too loud for her to call for help.

"Maybe la strega Americano would apologize for hurting Luigi, and come on back to my place. I promise I'll be gentle." He stuck his face right up to hers and she was sorely tempted to smack his oily grin right off of it.

She shifted away from him but he pressed himself toward her, wrapping his arm around her shoulder.

"I could teach you all sorts of things, la strega. Things you'd thank me for."

"Get your hands off of me," she shouted at him, just as she heard a loud crash and looked to see Luigi falling backward, the blackest of red wine streaming down his head and onto his body. She looked up to see Matteo, holding the glass neck of a wine bottle, the remaining chunks and shards of glass adorning Luigi's hair and clothing.

A crowd gathered around the scene as Luigi bled heavily from where Matteo broke the bottle of wine on his head. Matteo stood over the drunken farmer, calling for his brother to get the police.

"So he was your charitable host?" he said. "I should have known. The local women know to keep their distance from him. I hadn't realized he was enlisting free farm labor so he could molest them. We'll make sure that is the end of Luigi's despicable behavior.

"I don't think I've ever said this to anyone before but you're officially my hero, Signor Romeo."

"And you're officially my favorite unwitting victim of a disgusting dirtball of a local farmer, Signora Moretti."

Chapter Twenty-Two

Lizzie didn't realize how serious Valentina and Taylor were about shopping until she found herself piled high with bags while enjoying *aperitivo* at a bar off the Piazza della Signoria. Lizzie slowly drank her Aperol Spritz as they discussed their shopping booty did some people watching on the crowded piazza.

"You guys, I can't believe all the clothes you bought for me," Lizzie said. "What am I going to do with them once I leave?"

"How about just don't leave? That makes it easiest," Taylor said.

"Plus, it's the preferable thing to do," Valentina said. "Surrender to it."

Lizzie thought about that. Wasn't that what she said in her dreams that first night? *I surrender. Take me, I'm yours.*

Of course over the past several weeks, she'd given herself to Matteo more times than she could even count. Try as she might to think of good reasons to leave, she wasn't coming up with any. She really liked him, and they had fun together. He'd even let her help with the harvest on the last day. And yes, it was backbreaking work and, she was learning, particularly exhausting for her since rebounding from pneumonia wasn't the easiest thing to do.

"So what's the first thing you're going to wear?" Taylor asked.

Lizzie cocked an eyebrow. "The very first thing,

without question, will be the La Perla lace garter belt and stockings." She grinned. "Have to play to my audience."

"I'm so glad you and Matteo are having fun," Valentina said. "I just knew you two would hit it off."

"I didn't," Lizzie said. "He was such a meanie when he found me that first morning."

"Yeah, but he's a big teddy bear, my big brother is." Valentina grinned. "He'd no sooner abandon a woman in need than kill someone's pet puppy."

"He's a keeper, no doubt about it," Taylor said.

They talked and laughed, joking about some of the strange street performers like the men who pretended to levitate.

"I don't know how I can repay you for your generosity," Lizzie said. "And really, I can't. I probably have about two hundred dollars in my bank account."

They held up their hands in refusal. "Our gift to you. Thanks for getting Matteo out of his funk."

As they held their drinks up to toast, a boy of about ten ran up and grabbed Taylor's purse from the table and ran quickly into the thick throng of people.

"Hey, stop that boy!" Lizzie said as she stood and instinctively ran after him. What the hell? Luckily she was wearing a pair of leather flats and not those crazy high heels the other two had on; she could pivot and dodge and not break an ankle. She pushed people out of the way, routing here and there as the boy darted between people's legs. Suddenly she noticed a car baring the words carabinieri, the Italian military police one often sees in cities.

Her Italian was so weak, but she had a few words in it. "*Aiuto! Polizia! Prontissimo!*" she said, pointing toward the little urchin still clutching the expensive black designer satchel. The boy looped back in the direction of the two women, who shouted someone to catch him, and just as Lizzie started to run out of steam, she made one last attempt, grabbing for the boy's ankle and pulling him down.

The police arrived on her heels, and she left them to deal with the boy while she returned the purse to Taylor.

"Holy crap," she said. "Didn't you say you're getting over pneumonia?"

Lizzie shrugged. "I wasn't going to let that kid get away with it."

"You, my dear, are seriously hard core. You'll fit in just fine with the Romeos."

Chapter Twenty-Three

LIZZIE was the hero at dinner. Even Sandro felt compelled to thank her.

"I'd like to make a toast to Lizzie," he said. "I know I was unfairly judgmental, and for that I apologize, but you all know I can be a bit of a hothead."

Everyone laughed. No exaggeration there.

"But thank you for helping out my beloved Taylor when she was in need. You've taught me an important lesson about being there for others and not expecting the worst.

"You really should have had that recorded," Matteo whispered in her ear. "You'll likely never hear those words uttered from his lips again."

She pointed to her head. "It's all in here. I can go back and remember it anytime I want."

"Can you remember what I taught you about picking grapes?"

"Yeah, yeah. Treat them gently, like a lover. Or was it punish the vine, pamper the clusters, where you push on the canes at the same time to get a better position to pull out the bunches of grapes. It sounds a little kinky, though, when you think about it."

"If you give me a chance after dinner, I'd love to try to pamper your clusters, baby."

She giggled and everyone looked at them. Little did they know Sandro was still droning on.

"And I owe apologies to each and every one of you," he said. "I know I was too domineering, and I made you all feel like you didn't have a good role here to grow into. That was my mistake, and my fiancée has pointed that out to me in no uncertain terms."

"Fiancée?" Valentina and Lizzie both said in unison. Fabiana came out of the kitchen carrying another dish. "Who's engaged?"

Taylor stood up next to Sandro and held out her hand for everyone to see the beautiful ruby stone surrounded by diamonds. The women all squealed and hugged her, and the men patted Sandro on the back and hugged Taylor too. "I may have mentioned to Sandro that I would be ready to marry him if he could show me he's trying to be a kinder, gentler big brother. Because, well, let's face it, you all know he means well. He's just sometimes lousy at getting his message out there."

"Gee, ya think?" Matteo whispered to Lizzie who shushed him.

"And I'm going to sit down with each of you to start working on a long-term strategy for the Romeo family. Perhaps I can take a much-needed break, and maybe you can finally take on some responsibilities around this place." He gave them all a wry wink. "Starting first with Matteo, who I think might be just the person, with his wanderlust, to take charge of overseas sales for Romeo wines. You'll have complete dominion over this area of the company and you can come and go as you please. And I promise I'll mind my own business. Completely."

Lizzie nodded at that and looked at Matteo. "This seems like a dream come true for you. Now you can travel to your heart's content and not have Sandro flipping out on you."

He nodded. "It's an interesting idea," he said. "I'll have to think on it."

"Think on it? What's to think on?"

Matteo shrugged. Little did he want to scare her off by saying he didn't want to be away from her so often. It was going to be hard enough when she left, but for them to be separated by continents? He hated the idea more than he could admit.

Chapter Twenty-Four

"**YOU** want to take a walk?" Matteo said to Lizzie.

"Sure, I think I'm up for it." The race to stop the thief had really sucked it out of her and for the past few days, she'd slept much of each day away. If only she could have Matteo by her side all day long, it would have been more enjoyable recovery time. But at this time of year, it wasn't possible.

They followed a footpath through the sunflower fields, up and over a hill, and stopped at a grove of old-growth olive trees.

"The olive harvest will likely begin next week," Matteo said.

"Do you guys make a party of that too?"

"We make a party of just about anything." He laughed. "And we'll figure out a religious ceremony to tack on alongside it just for good measure."

"At least it will be a Luigi-free celebration."

"You know, sometimes I come out here for perspective," he said, pointing to the strong, gnarled trees whose trunks and limbs had witnessed history for even longer than the Romeos had been making wine. "Some of these trees are over a thousand years old. They've seen invaders conquered and vanquished, have seen lovers quarrel and make love. They've seen life and death, in all of its beautiful messiness."

"I didn't know trees had so many human

characteristics," Lizzie said. "Nor did I realize people could actually make love at the base of an olive tree—a lot of suckers shooting up, and those roots, they'd dig in."

"If you're lucky, one of these days I'll show you how to have amazing olive grove sex."

"It can't hold a candle to bathtub sex."

"Or shower sex," he said. "I think that was nothing to sneer at."

She leaned over and kissed him. "Up against the wall, the water running down me. I liked it."

They stopped to kiss longer.

"Have you given any more thought to Sandro's proposal?" she said. "It sounds like the perfect opportunity for someone who loves to travel."

He cocked his brow. "Precisely what I've been thinking," he said. "Know anyone like that?"

"I could think of one or two people, maybe."

"Ritz or Four Seasons?"

"Depends," she said. "Which has the bigger bathtub?"

"Then the answer is yes," Matteo said. "With you along for the journey, how could I ever say no?"

Thank you so much for reading
Black Sheep Romeo!
I hope you enjoyed it! If so, please help others find this book:

1. Help other people find this book by writing a review.

2. Sign up for my new releases email so you can find out about the next book as soon as it's available and get fun giveaways.
   http://eepurl.com/baaewn

3. Like my Facebook page.
   www.facebook.com/jennygardinerbooks

And I love to hear from readers! Let me know what you think about my books! You can write to me at jenny@jennygardiner.net, and visit me on the web at www.jennygardiner.net.

Turn the page for a sneak peek of the next book in The Royal Romeos – **Red Carpet Romeo!**

Red Carpet Romeo

The Lord Chamberlain is commanded by the Queen of Monaforte to invite
Valentina Letizia Beatrice Romeo
To the Marriage of
His Royal Highness, Prince Luca Francesco DeMaio, Duke of Bartolomea
With
Miss Larkin Mallory
At the Cathedral of Santo Giacomo il Maggiore
On Friday, December 20, at 5:00 p.m.

A reply is requested to: State Invitations Secretary, Lord Chamberlain's Office,
Grande Palace of Monaforte,
Porto Castello, Monaforte
Dress: Uniform or white tie attire requested

TEN YEARS AGO

VALENTINA Romeo learned early in life that in order to survive you had to be tough. As the only girl surrounded by six testosterone-laden brothers, she had to be loud to be heard, and—no shrinking violet—believe her, she wanted to be heard.

But it wasn't easy, because her brothers were mostly bigger and stronger and liked to put her in her place, which meant Valentina was too often left itching for a fight. How dare those boys tell her she couldn't climb those ancient olive trees with them? And who were they to tell her she couldn't descend into the damp caves on the family estate and go exploring where it was rumored German soldiers hid at the end of World War II? Time and again those boys left her in their dust and feeling bitter that no matter how hard she tried to be one of them, they fought her ever inch of the way.

Of course in their defense they had some competing interests: regular threats from their parents to take care of their "delicate" sister and protect her not only from outside forces but also from her overly ambitious, tomboyish self meant they were constantly conflicted. They knew if they brought Valentina with them when they went off to pursue their near-daily explorations and investigations on the vast tracts of farm and forested hills on which the Romeo family had been growing grapes and olives for six hundred years, they'd be responsible for anything that could go wrong. And what boy in his right mind wanted to carry that burden?

For a respite from this frustrating daily conflict, Valentina looked forward to summertime, when her family joined with their cousins, the royal family from neighboring Monaforte, at a huge seaside compound on the Ligurian sea in Northern Italy. There the many cousins spent their days on the beach building sand forts and castles—something they were intimately familiar with—and digging for shells and fossils and swimming until they could swim no longer. It was a paradise for children, and while Valentina certainly enjoyed keeping company with her only female cousin, Isabella, it was her older cousin Luca who immediately dazzled her.

Luca, who treated her like an equal even though she was six years younger. Luca who made certain to include his young cousin when the kids hiked up high into the Ligurian hills to capture the view of the sea for miles around them. Luca who caught a salamander and named it Valentina in his cousin's honor. That was all it took for Valentina to be smitten for life: if she could harbor a crush on a blood relative, well she would have. Instead, she just adored him and cherished the time they got to spend together.

And then when she was fourteen, Luca showed up that summer with a new friend—a roommate from university. Only then did Valentina understand how a girl could swoon over a handsome man. Because Parker Hornsby, with his sandy blond hair, twinkly blue eyes, dimpled cheeks and brilliant white smile, was indeed swoon-worthy.

"Valentina," Luca said as he swooped to hug his cousin and kiss both her cheeks as was customary. "I missed you so much." He squeezed her nose affectionately. "I want you to meet my friend Parker Hornsby. He's from America. I told him what a magical place Cieli di Zaffiro was." Sapphire Skies: it would then become known as the place where she first fell in love.

Valentina took one look at her cousin's new friend and was thunderstruck. Something deep in her gut roiled to life, something she'd yet to recognize, a feeling so powerful it made her scared and happy and nervous and worried, all wrapped up into one untidy heap of swirling emotions that about did her in, they terrified her so.

"Nice to meet you," Parker said, extending his hand to Valentina, which completely threw her off. She'd expected the usual greeting, a kiss on one cheek and then a kiss on the other. So instead of reaching her arm out to shake his hand, she leaned in as if to field his courteous side kisses, and instead his hand jammed into her barely-there breasts and she about died from embarrassment as everyone standing nearby laughed at the mix-up, and so immediately she fled the room, mortified.

When Luca came up to check on her later, her tear-stained cheeks thoroughly betrayed her lackluster attempt at feigning indifference.

"Valentina ballerina," he said, scruffing her long dark hair with his fingers. It was her favorite nickname, one only he used with her. It didn't even make sense, because she was so far removed from being a delicate ballerina, he should have called her out for the tomboy she was. Give her a soccer ball and she'd kick pretty much anyone's ass. A pair of ballet slippers? She'd probably slide them on her hands thinking they were mittens. "Why the long face, my friend?"

Valentina sat on the edge of the bed, swinging her legs and kicking the side of the bed in rhythmic motion, staring out the window, lips pursed, not making eye contact with her cousin.

"What happened that made you run off like you did?"

Luca said, pressing her for more details.

Valentina hung her head, so embarrassed. "Nothing," she said.

"Nothing?" He frowned and arched his brow, his bright blue eyes twinkling.

"All right. Fine," she said with a huff. "I thought he was going to kiss my cheeks like everyone does and instead he reached out his arm and his hand hit my chest and God, Luca, I mean, really—"

"Oh, sweetie," he said. "Nobody even saw that."

"Of course they did. They all laughed."

"They just laughed at the confusion of the thing. No one was laughing at you, and no one noticed if his hand even touched you."

She crossed her arms over said chest, about which she'd become acutely self-conscious, what with all of the other girls her age having blossomed into B-cup babes by then, while Valentina was still about as flat as the field of sunflowers her parents had planted for her brother Matteo near their manor home. The last thing she wanted was anyone making cracks about that virtual concavity resting atop her chest.

"Hey," he said, leaning forward and coaxing her chin with his pointer finger so she was facing him. "It's okay, Valentina. Believe me, we all adore you to the moon and back."

She frowned. "It's just that, well, Luca, I'm a teenager, and look at me." She swept her hands along her t-shirt clad chest, which was sporting a bra out of pure youthful desire, certainly not need.

Her cousin reached around and wrapped her in a bear hug. "Oh, sweetie. Trust me, you are perfect just the way you are. And believe me, before you know it, this is going to be the least of your problems. Pretty soon we'll be beating the boys away, they're going to be pounding down the doors just to get to you. Don't you worry your pretty little head any more, okay? Besides, you'll always be my Valentina ballerina."

It took Valentina a few days but eventually she started actually speaking to Parker Hornsby, and that swirling mess of confusing feelings soon crystallized into what was irrefutable in her young mind: love. She was indeed convinced she was in love with Luca's good friend, who was handsome and athletic and oh, the timbre of his voice was like hearing the very church bells she'd imagined would peal on their wedding day.

Besides, he always picked her for his side when they played pick-up soccer on the beach, so she knew the feelings were mutual. But as the summer days progressed, she yearned desperately to somehow advance beyond the stage of goal assists and into something more intimate, like a first kiss. She even practiced her nascent kissing skills on a stuffed monkey she slept with, for the day it would come in handy. She had no idea how she would drum up the nerve to act, but she knew she had to; she'd never forgive herself if she let him get away.

One night the cousins built a huge bonfire on the beach. They sat around talking and laughing, the older ones drinking wine and some even went swimming. Valentina sat along the shore, her chin to her knees, not particularly interested in going into the dark ocean water. Until Parker reached out his hand to her.

"Let's go, short stuff," he said to her, clasping her hand in his as he pulled her toward the water. At first she shook her head, refusing, but, hey, he was holding her hand! How could she say no? She lifted herself off the cold sand and followed him into the surf, laughing and splashing and thoroughly elated because she knew this must the sign she was waiting for.

She tripped and fell in the shallows, and he leaned forward to help her up. Just as he reached for her, she wrapped her arms around his neck, blurted out those three fateful words—I love you—while awkwardly angling her mouth to his and planting her lips on his as if she was administering mouth-to-mouth resuscitation to a training dummy.

Parker, instead of embracing her advances, pushed her away.

"Valentina, no!" he said, raking his hand through his hair, clearly put off by her declaration and unwanted advances.

She looked at him with querying eyes, her brow wrinkled, confused at his rejection. "But I thought you liked me," she said.

He shook his head, looking around, which she took to mean he was embarrassed if anyone had just seen what had transpired. "Of course I like you as my friend's cousin," he said. "But you're just a young girl. This," he said, pointing back and forth between the two of them, "will never happen, Valentina. I'm a grown-up and you're a child." With that, he turned and raced toward the older boys, leaving her dazed and heartbroken in the cold nighttime tide pool, her eyes filled with tears.

He was right, she thought. That would never happen. Because she had too much self-respect to moon over that jerk. But she vowed that day she would no longer be the tomboy buddy to all the guys; she was going to show people like that rotten Parker Hornsby. One day men like him would be swooning over her. That she was going to make good and sure of.

Red Carpet Romeo

coming February 17, 2017.

About the Author

Jenny Gardiner is the author of #1 Kindle Bestseller *Slim to None* and the award-winning novel *Sleeping with Ward Cleaver*. Her latest works are the *It's Reigning Men* series, featuring *Something in the Heir*; *Heir Today Gone Tomorrow*; *Bad to the Throne; Love is in the Heir*; *Shame of Thrones*; *Throne for a Loop; It's Getting Hot in Heir; A Court Gesture;* and her new Royal Romeos series, featuring *Red-Hot Romeo; Black Sheep Romeo* and the upcoming *Red Carpet Romeo.* She also published the memoir *Winging It: A Memoir of Caring for a Vengeful Parrot Who's Determined to Kill Me,* now re-titled *Bite Me: a Parrot, a Family and a Whole Lot of Flesh Wounds*; the novels *Anywhere but Here*; *Where the Heart Is*; the essay collection *Naked Man on Main Street*, and *Accidentally on Purpose* and *Compromising Positions* (writing as Erin Delany); and is a contributor to the humorous dog anthology *I'm Not the Biggest Bitch in This Relationship*.

Her work has been found in Ladies Home Journal, the Washington Post, Marie-Claire.com, and on NPR's Day to Day. She was also a columnist for Charlottesville's Daily Progress for over a decade, and is the Volunteer Coordinator for the Virginia Film Festival.

She has worked as a professional photographer, an orthodontic assistant (learning quite readily that she was not cut out for a career in polyester), a waitress (probably her highest-paying job), a TV reporter, a pre-obituary writer, as well as a publicist to a United States Senator (where she first learned to write fiction). She's photographed Prince Charles (and her assistant husband got him to chuckle!), Elizabeth Taylor, and the president of Uganda. She and her family and menagerie of pets now live a less exotic life in Virginia.

Visit Jenny at her website at www.jennygardiner.net where you can sign up for her newsletter, visit her blog, or find her on Facebook and Twitter. And every blue moon she'll post adorable pictures of her pets on Instagram as @thejennygardiner.